CARNEGIE MEDAL

1982   Mahy, Margaret

The Haunting

The Haunting

MARGARET MAHY

The Haunting

A MARGARET K. McELDERRY BOOK

Atheneum   1984   New York

Library of Congress Cataloging in Publication Data

Mahy, Margaret.
The haunting.

"A Margaret K. McElderry book."
SUMMARY: After a shy and rather withdrawn eight-year-
old begins receiving frightening supernatural images
and messages, he learns about a family legacy which
could be considered a curse or a rare gift.
[1. Extrasensory perception—Fiction. 2. Super-
natural—Fiction] I. Title.
PZ7.M2773 Hau   [Fic]   82-3983
ISBN 0-689-50243-5   AACR2
Copyright © 1982 by Margaret Mahy
Printed and bound by Fairfield Graphics
Fairfield, Pennsylvania
First Printing, August 1982
Second Printing, February 1983
Third Printing, April 1983
Fourth Printing, November 1983
Fifth Printing March 1984

Contents

The Haunting

1

Barnaby's Dead

When, suddenly, on an ordinary Wednesday, it seemed to Barney that the world tilted and ran downhill in all directions, he knew he was about to be haunted again. It had happened when he was younger but he had thought that being haunted was a babyish thing that you grew out of, like crying when you fell over, or not having a bike.

"Remember Barney's imaginary friends, Mantis, Bigbuzz and Ghost?" Claire — his stepmother — sometimes said. "The garden seems empty now that they've gone. I quite miss them."

But she was really pleased perhaps because, being so very real to Barney, they had become too real for her to laugh over. Barney had been sorry to lose them, but he wanted Claire to feel comfortable living with him. He could not remember his own mother and Claire had come as a wonderful surprise, giving him a hug when he came home from school, asking him about his day, telling him about hers, arranging picnics and unexpected parties and helping him with hard homework. It seemed worth losing Mantis, Bigbuzz and Ghost and the other kind phantoms that had been his friends for so many days before Claire came.

Yet here it was beginning again . . . the faint

dizzy twist in the world around him, the thin singing drone as if some tiny insect were trapped in the curling mazes of his ear. Barney looked up at the sky searching for a ghost but there was only a great blueness like a weight pressing down on him. He looked away quickly, half expecting to be crushed into a sort of rolled-out gingerbread boy in an enormous stretched-out school uniform. Then he saw his ghost on the footpath beside him.

A figure was slowly forming out of the air: a child — quite a little one, only about four or five — struggling to be real. A curious pale face grew clearer against a halo of shining hair, silver gold hair that curled and crinkled, fading into the air like bright smoke. The child was smiling. It seemed to be having some difficulty in seeing Barney so that he felt that *he* might be the one who was not quite real. Well, he was used to feeling that. In the days before Claire he had often felt that he himself couldn't be properly heard or seen. But then Mantis had taken time to become solid and Ghost had always been dim and smoky. So Barney was not too surprised to see the ghost looking like a flat paper doll stuck against the air by some magician's glue. Then it became round and real, looking alive, but old-fashioned and strange, in its blue velvet suit and lace collar. A soft husky voice came out of it.

"Barnaby's dead!" it said. "Barnaby's dead! I'm going to be very lonely."

Barney stood absolutely still, feeling more tilted and dizzy than ever. His head rang as if it were strung

2

like a bead on the thin humming that ran, like electricity, from ear to ear.

The ghost seemed to be announcing his death by his proper christened name of Barnaby — not just telling him he was going to die, but telling him that he was actually dead already. Now it spoke again.

"Barnaby's dead!" it said in exactly the same soft husky voice. "Barnaby's dead! I'm going to be very lonely." It wasn't just that it said the same words that it had said earlier. Its very tone — the lifts and falls and flutterings of its voice — was exactly the same. If it had added, "This is a recorded message," it would not have seemed very out of place. Barney wanted to say something back to it, but what can you say to a ghost? You can't joke with it. Perhaps you could ask it questions, but Barney was afraid of the answers this ghost might give him. He would have to believe what it told him, and it might tell him something terrible.

As it turned out this ghost was not one that would answer questions anyway. It had only one thing to say, and it had said it. It began to swing from side to side, like an absent-minded compass needle searching for some lost North. Its shape did not change but it swung widely and lay crossways in the air looking silly, but also very frightening.

"Barnaby's dead!" it said, "Barnaby's dead! And I'm going to be very lonely." Then it spun like a propeller, slowly at first then faster and faster until it was only a blur of silver-gold in the air. It spun faster still until even the colours vanished and there was nothing but a faint clear flicker. Then it stopped and the ordinary air closed over it. The humming in Barney's ears stopped, the world straightened out; time began again, the wind blew, trees moved, cars droned and tooted. Down through the air from the point where the ghost had disappeared fluttered a cloud of blue flakes. Barney caught a few of them in his hand. For a moment he held nothing but scraps of paper from a torn-up picture! He caught a glimpse of a blue velvet sleeve, a piece of lace cuff and a pink thumb and finger. Then the paper turned into quick-silver beads of colour that ran through his fingers and were lost before they fell on to the footpath.

Barney wanted to be at home at once. He did not want the in-between time of going down streets and around corners. There were no short cuts. He had to run all the way, fearing that at any moment he might be struck by lightning, or a truck, or by some terrible dissolving sickness that would eat him away as he ran. Little stumbles in his running made him think he might have been struck by bullets. His hair felt prickly and he wondered if it was turning white. He could imagine arriving at home and seeing his face in the hall mirror staring out under hair like cotton wool. He could imagine Claire saying, "Barney, what on earth have you been up to? Look at the state of your hair." How could he say, "Well, there was this ghost telling me that I was dead." Claire would just say sternly, "Barney, have you been reading horror comics again?"

As it happened it was not Claire who met him when he got home but his two sisters, one on either side of the doorway — his thin knobbly sister Troy, stormy in her black cloud of hair, her black eyebrows almost meeting over her long nose, and brown, round Tabitha, ready to talk and talk as she always did.

"Where have you been?" she asked. "You're late and have missed out on family news. But it's ok — the family novelist will now bring you up to date." By "the family novelist" Tabitha meant herself. She was writing the world's greatest novel, but no one was allowed to read it until she was twenty-one and it was published. However, she talked about it all the time and showed off by taking pages and pages of notes and talking about those, too.

"I stopped to . . ." Barney began. He felt his voice quaver and die out. He couldn't tell Tabitha about his ghost, particularly in front of Troy who was five years older than he was and silent and scornful. But anyway — Tabitha was not interested in his explanations. She was too busy telling him the family news in her own way.

"We are a house of mourning," she said in an important voice. "One of our dear relations has died. It's really good material for my novel and I'm taking notes like anything. No one I know has ever died before."

Barney stared at her in horror.

"Not Claire!" he began to say because he was always afraid that they would lose Claire in some way, particularly now that she was expecting a baby which Barney knew was dangerous work. But Tabitha was not upset enough for it to be Claire.

"Great-Uncle Barnaby . . . a Scholar relation," she went on and then, as Barney's face stiffened and became blank she added, sarcastically, "You do remember him don't you? You're named after him."

"I'm going to be very lonely," said a soft, husky voice in Barney's ear. He felt the world begin to slide away.

"Hey!" Troy's voice spoke on his other side. "You don't have to be upset. He was old . . . and he'd been ill — very ill, for a while."

"It's not that!" Barney stammered. "I — I thought it might be me."

"Lonely!" said the echo in his haunted ear.

"I thought it *was* me," Barney said, and suddenly the world made up its mind and shrank away from him, grown to tennis ball size, then walnut size, then a pinhead of brightness in whirling darkness. On the steps of his own home Barney had fainted.

2

The Lost Great-Uncle

Barney's faint was only a very little one. Within a few minutes he was in his room having his forehead bathed by Troy and with Claire holding a glass of water to his lips. Tabitha watched with interest. Now she was over the fright of having her brother fall limp and pale at her feet she became very businesslike about it all.

"I might never get another chance like this," she told anyone who could be bothered listening as she moved to study Barney from a different angle. "We're such a healthy family, the chance of anyone fainting in the next ten years is absolutely nil And my novel will be published by then."

"You silly old thing!" said Claire gently to Barney. "Just lie still for a bit, there's a good boy. You're looking better already." She set out to make life enjoyable for him, put a fresh flowery pillowcase on his pillow, made Tabitha and her notebook go grumbling out of the room, and then went out herself to make him a lemon drink. Barney thought about pretending to be sicker than he was just for the pleasure of being looked after. It seemed a bit baby-ish, but after all, before Claire had come he had not had much kindness and fussing so surely he was allowed to make up for it now.

However, he looked and felt so much better by dinner time that, when Claire said he could get up if he wanted to, he did, and that was enjoyable too, for Claire sat him in the most comfortable chair, covered him over with a rug and gave him his dinner on a tray. Everyone else was having meat and vegetables but Barney had an egg especially poached to a beautiful yellow and white on a thick slice of hot, buttered toast. He was having all the fun of being an invalid without actually being sick. Sometimes his mind flicked back to the blue velvet ghost and then pulled away sharply. It was like no other haunting he could ever remember. Even now it seemed as if somewhere in just-past time some other Barney was still standing, staring at that smiling pale child and still hearing the husky voice repeating its odd message.

"Fancy our Barney fainting!" said Barney's father. "You must have been thinking too hard at school, Barney."

"If people fainted because of too much thinking I'd scarcely ever be conscious," Tabitha began at once. "I think and think all the time, and I've never fainted — not once." She looked over at Barney enviously. "Why do the best things always happen to other people and not to a promising writer?"

"If people fainted from too much talking . . ." began Troy and then fell silent. Seven words were a lot for Troy to say all at once like that.

"It could be the hot day — though it wasn't very hot," Claire said, "or shock of some sort, or just tiredness . . . The doctor didn't seem too worried."

Tabitha smiled in a superior way as if she knew a great deal more about fainting than a mere doctor.

"People are supposed to faint if they get sudden bad news . . . if a girl friend is killed in front of their very eyes or they lose their money or something. Barney hasn't got a girl friend — not that we know of — and he hasn't got much money because I know where he keeps it and I counted it last week. There's not enough to be worth fainting over. And it can't be the great-uncle dying, can it? I mean Barney didn't know him much."

"Barney's a sensitive boy," Claire said thoughtfully.

"But he said that he thought it was *him* — he-himself-Barney — who was dead, didn't he, Troy?"

"Yes!" agreed Troy, staring at Barney as if he were a riddle and she might work out his answer.

"It was a pretty funny thing to say," Tabitha went on. "He said, 'I thought it was me,' twice, and then he just keeled over. I've got it written down in my notebook. I might get you to sign it later, Barn, just to prove it. You won't mind, will you?"

"Honestly, Tabitha, the sooner your novel is written and published the better," Claire said crisply, seeing Barney was being made uncomfortable by these comments. "No more talking about Barney's faint. He's better now — that's the main thing "

"Ok — let's talk about funerals," Tabitha replied at once.

Settling back into the big chair Barney felt comfortable again. There was no way he could have explained about the ghost or its repeated message. No one would have believed him and he did not like remembering such strangeness. Partly to get over the memory of it he looked at his family, appreciating their usualness — his father, John, tall and rather bald, giving him an anxious glance and then grinning as their eyes met, Claire with her fair hair tied back from her face with a blue scarf, smiling around the table, Tabitha, fat and golden brown, and frowning Troy who seemed to move around in the heart of her own private storm, struggling against tempests no one else could see. They did not change or float in the air and vanish. They stayed still and were always themselves.

"Can we go to the great-uncle's funeral, Dad?" asked Tabitha. "I've never been to a funeral before. We're allowed time off school for funerals and I'll tell you what — if I go I won't write any notes until I get home and no one's watching."

"No!" her father said, very firmly. "I might go but there's no need for the rest of you to be there. Though I think we should call in on your Grandfather and Grandmother Scholar, not to mention your great-grandmother sometime in the weekend . . . tomorrow afternoon, say."

"I say 'No' to that!" Tabitha cried at once. "Visiting that great-grandmother is too much like visiting some witch who has lost her magic, but kept her nastiness. Let's just stay at home and send them a card."

"Tabby, that's not very nice," Claire said reprovingly.

10

"Well, *she's* not very nice," Tabitha argued. "Visiting her is like having a long refreshing drink of vinegar."

Barney, Tabitha and Troy had three sets of grandparents. There were their father's parents, the Palmers, whom they had always known and whom they visited every Christmas or New Year, and there were Claire's parents, the Martins, who were new grandparents and whom they saw nearly every week and certainly on birthdays. But in between these families was another set of relations, a spare set as it were. There were Grandpa and Grandma Scholar, the parents of Dove, the children's dead mother, and there were a few great-uncles: Great-Uncle Guy, Great-Uncle Alberic and Great-Uncle Barnaby, now dead. There was also a great-grandmother — Great-Granny Scholar — a terrible old lady, a small, thin witch, frail but furious.

"She's probably very nice once you get to know her," Claire said firmly.

"Not her!" Tabitha said cheerfully. "I don't mind seeing Grandpa and Grandma Scholar — they're nice — but I can't stand Great-Granny with those little fierce eyes and all those wrinkles."

"She can't help being wrinkled," her father said. "She's very old really, close on ninety." But he did not sound as if he minded hearing Tabitha's criticism.

"I don't mind her being wrinkled," Tabitha replied in surprise. "It's just that all her wrinkles are so angry. She's like a wall with furious swear words scribbled all over it."

11

This was exactly what Barney thought, but he stayed silent. In the years before Claire had married their father, silence had become a habit with Barney, particularly as Tabitha seemed determined to take up all the talking time. Perhaps that was why Troy was so silent, too.

"I don't think I've ever met her," Claire said thoughtfully. "Nor the great-uncles either for that matter — well, only very briefly — so I can't give an opinion."

"I've got a picture," Troy observed. "A photograph! Of the uncles, that is."

"That photograph!" Her father looked pleased. "Have you got it handy, Troy? Run and fetch it."

For a moment Troy looked as if she might argue. Then she pushed her chair back and went off down the hall to her room. When she came back she had the photograph with her.

Her father showed it to Claire.

"That's Grandpa!" he said. "Ben! And that's Alberic, isn't it?"

"Guy," Troy corrected him.

"Guy, then. He's the doctor. Well *that* must be Alberic, and that's Barnaby."

"What about the little one!" Claire asked as her husband hesitated.

"I don't remember his name," he said. "He's dead! At least I think he's dead. He grew up to be rather a black sheep — ran away from home and was never heard of again. That sort of thing!"

Tabitha was delighted.

"What a day!" she exclaimed. "Things have been going on, boring, boring, boring, and then all of a sudden a death and a faint and a lost great-uncle. I didn't know we had an extra one, did you, Troy? Perhaps he isn't dead and one day he'll turn up really rich and loaded with presents. He could be a millionaire by now. In a book he would be."

"There *was* something funny about him," mused her father. "One of those — you know — not-to-be-talked-about-things, and no one *did* talk about it, so I've never found out what it was. I don't think Dove knew herself. Nothing disgraceful or catching: nothing you'd inherit . . . just mysterious."

"He may not have had anything disgraceful you'd inherit," Claire studied the photograph carefully, "but someone *did* inherit something, all the same. He looks just like our Barney. Or rather Barney looks just like him."

"Barney can't see! Let Barney see," Tabitha cried generously. "Look Barn . . . the four main great-uncles plus the lost, odd, mysterious, runaway, little, new great-uncle, with nothing disgraceful or catching, except that he looks like you."

Barney only half wanted to see the photograph. He had to command his hand to reach out and take it gingerly

Four tall young men and one boy! Like ghosts, the old faces of the present great-uncles could be seen haunting the faces of the young great-uncles in the photograph. Uncle Barnaby, whose name had been passed to Barney, looked out, smiling a fifty-five-year-old smile at him. Great-Uncles Guy and Alberic, and Grandpa Scholar too, all smiled the tired, patient smiles they still had. But the smallest great-uncle of all looked away at the side of the picture He seemed to be standing a little apart from the others, added in carelessly at the last minute, the photographer not caring much whether he was looking at the camera or not. Barney was very relieved . He had been afraid that he might recognize this unknown great-uncle, but he did not. Perhaps the great-uncle did not look like him, he couldn't be sure of that, but he could be sure of one thing . . . he wasn't wearing a velvet suit and he did not have a head of fair curls.

"A lost great-uncle!" Tabitha repeated, unwilling to let this sensation go. "Terrific!"

"I don't see why," her father objected. "None of us is ever likely to meet him."

"At least he's *there*," Tabitha pointed out. "We're mostly so ordinary with our car and our lawn-mower and things. I want life to be a lot more mysterious than that. Didn't Mother ever say anything to you about him — anything at all — just one single thing that you can remember?"

"Nothing but what I've told you," her father declared ."No — hang on a moment. I do remember once asking just *what* was wrong with this chap and Dove laughed and said he had a golden piece in his mind. Make what you can of that!"

It was plain to see that Tabitha would make a lot of it.

"That's great!" she breathed. "Can't I just take

14

one note, Claire, before I forget?"

"You won't forget that," Claire assured her.

"I like things written down,"Tabitha mumbled.

"Then you've got them for good."

Later, when Barney was in bed, not thinking of great-uncles, dead or alive or even mislaid, not even thinking of the ghost, he felt something strange begin in his mind . . . a kind of stirring and opening as if some butterfly were struggling out of its chrysalis and trying to unfold crumpled wings.

A picture was trying to form, a face was trying to make itself seen. As soon as he opened his eyes it vanished, but when he closed them once more the unfolding patiently began all over again.

Barney was not alarmed. There was none of the dizziness, none of the droning that had announced the appearance of the blue velvet ghost. It felt more like one of those dreams that come before you are properly asleep. Watching, as the face struggled towards him, it seemed to him that it reminded him of someone but he couldn't think who.

Just before he dropped into sleep, soft as a hand stroking the pillow beside his ear, a voice spoke.

"Are you there?" it said. "Are you there, Barnaby?"

But it was very faint and far away. Barney did not reply. His closed eyelids were still, and the voice was just another one of the voices of the people and animals that stalked the boundaries of his dreams.

3

In the Shadows

The next day began by being beautiful with its sky a pure and peaceful blue, the air warm but sparkling. Summer shimmered softly across the hills in folds of yellow.

Barney felt Saturday soak into his bones even before he woke up properly. The dreams of the night were forgotten, though the fact of the ghost was still there of course like a bruise in his memory. He went back to it, just to see how it felt and did not like it much, but it was over, like a bad day at school. You could only make up your mind to forget such things. When he came out looking for his breakfast, Claire looked him over carefully and then smiled, so he must have seemed all right. She had her hair in a long braid which was quite nice, but he liked it better when she put it up and looked more motherish. The braid made her seem less special, more like yet another sister in the family. Tabitha was talking, telling herself — and anyone who was interested — what she was going to do with her Saturday.

"First, jobs! Make bed, tidy room — all that sort of stuff," she declared. "Then — swimming pool! I expect I'll be there more or less all day, except I *could* come home for lunch but wouldn't it be easier for you, Claire, if I bought a pie and chips and Coke and just stayed there?"

"Fattening!" said Troy, looking at Tabitha's round face and plump arms.

"If I don't mind being fat, I don't see why other people should feel they've got to mind for me," Tabitha replied cheerfully. "And pies have got *some* food value — they've got vitamins or something, haven't they, Claire?"

"Protein," Troy replied. "A bit of protein, that's all. And Coke doesn't have anything in it except sweet carbohydrates."

"All this is by the way," Claire said, "because you're going to have to come home anyway, Tabitha. We're going to visit your Scholar grandparents this afternoon, just to pay our respects as they've lost Great-Uncle Barnaby."

"Oh no! Do we *have* to?" Tabitha screwed up her face as if in agony. "They're nice and all that! I do like them, but they're so sort of papery, if you know what I mean."

"How you do go on, Tabitha!" Claire replied. "It's very wearing. Look — they're your grandparents, and Great-Uncle Barnaby was your great-uncle, your grandfather's brother."

"Not good enough!" declared Tabitha. "Not enough reason to make us waste a Saturday afternoon just being polite."

"They like seeing us," said Troy.

"They must be mad!" exclaimed Tabitha. "None of us is beautiful. You're bony, I'm fat and Barney is like one of those ordinary brown dogs you see every-

where, nothing special. Of course you remember
them more than I do so it's probably not such a waste
of time for you." Tabitha marmaladed her toast in a
fretful way. "Suppose just Claire and Dad and you
and Barney go and I stay at the swimming pool
improving my diving? That's four-fifths polite.
Plenty!"

"Tabitha — stop it! You know you have to go,"
Claire said. "No arguments! I rang last night and said
we'd all go and see them. I don't want them to think
I'm trying to keep you all to myself. You still belong
to them too, you know."

"But it's just a sort of accident," whined Tabitha.
"Families are accidental. I mean — look at me, look
at Troy! Dead opposites really, and . . ."

"Tabitha," Claire cried, "I'm going to be steady
and stern with you. We are all — I repeat *all* — going
to visit the Scholars this afternoon. And now let's
change the subject. Barney — you're very quiet this
morning."

"There's no space to say anything when Tabitha's
around," Barney replied. "If I say something — well
I'm always talking at the same time as she is."

"It's not as if you ever have anything interesting
to say," Tabitha replied at once. "I mean, you're old
enough to speak but too young to have any brains.
You've only been interesting five times in your life —
no, six counting yesterday and — " Troy bumped
Tabitha on the head with her knuckles.

"Shut up!" she said, and Tabitha did, grinning
and quite pleased with herself though she had no

reason to be. Troy, standing behind her, looked over at Barney and waggled a toast crust at him as a sign of fellowship. Barney made a sign with his spoon, even though he couldn't help being curious about the five other times in his life he had interested Tabitha.

So in the afternoon, brushed and polished and sworn to behave well, bony Troy, fat Tabitha and brown, shy Barney were herded across the beautiful lawn that belonged to the house where Grandpa and Grandma Scholar lived.

The sitting room, with its blue carpet and flowery chairs and curtains, was full of people. Great-Uncles Alberic and Guy were there of course, tall, towering and toppling a little bit like elegant hollyhocks. There were some elderly family friends, all unknown to the Palmers, and sitting in the biggest chair of all, Great-Grandmother Scholar, even more scribbled on and screwed up by time than Barney had remembered her. She was absolutely neat, so neat that she seemed like a doll brought out of a glass case in a museum and sat up especially for the occasion. But her eyes were sharp and unfriendly, and her wrinkles were untidy — even wild as if time had played a careless game of tic-tac-toe all over her.

The great-uncles and the grandparents were really pleased to see them — there could be no mistake about that. They looked at the Palmer children so kindly and sadly and all gave the same sort of kiss, a light, dry, summery brush on the cheek. It was more like being kissed by trees than by people. But Great-Grandmother kissed them as if it were some-

19

thing disagreeable that *had* to be done, grim kisses in the centre of each forehead, and everything she said was disagreeable too. She looked up at Troy, whose face had become like an empty house, windows sealed, doors locked.

"There is no need to look so *sulky*, Troy," she said. "Sadness is reasonable at a time like this, but sulkiness is never acceptable." She looked at Tabitha and said, "Dear me — you have put on weight. Claire, this child should be on a strict diet. It can't be good to let her get as fat as all that." Tabitha turned away rolling her eyes so that people around smiled and tried to hide their smiles. However, she stood close by to watch while Barney was kissed.

"Dove's children!" Great-Granny Scholar said to someone standing behind Barney.

"And Daddy's, too!" Barney said. "And Claire's!" He would not let this witchy great-grandmother shut Claire out of his life, nor did he want to belong only to his dark, dead, mysterious mother.

"Dove died when this one was born," Great-Grandmother went on, as if he hadn't spoken. Then at last she looked at him properly. The whites of her eyes were yellowish. The brown irises were so dark he could not make out the pupil.

"I hope you're being a good boy these days."

"He's very good," Claire said. "A real jewel of a boy!"

"Too good really!" exclaimed Tabitha seeing a chance to give an opinion, "though he's mostly good by being quiet. People think being good and being quiet are the same thing in children." Everyone turned to stare at her and listen, which she enjoyed.

"She doesn't get that tongue from the Scholars," someone said, and laughed.

"For instance," Tabitha said quickly, "Barney's so good that when he heard Great-Uncle Barnaby had died he fainted right away on the steps. He wasn't sick or anything — just being sensitive like some child in an old-fashioned book."

"Tabitha — " said Claire warningly, "as far as you're concerned goodness and quietness *are* the same thing, believe me." And she pulled Tabitha back from the armchair with a firm hand. Great-Granny Scholar was still looking at Barney, but something in her gaze had altered. There was a new kind of sharpness in it, the sudden arrested sharpness of a cat that sees some sort of movement beginning in the shadows. Her mouth drew up, tightly wrinkled around the edges.

"Mother," said Grandfather Scholar, "may we get you a cup of tea? Janet has just made a big potful." (Janet was Grandma Scholar.)

The old lady turned away from Barney with a little sigh and he was free to go.

Grandmother Scholar and Great-Uncle Guy came over and suggested that Tabitha might like to help pass sandwiches and cakes around.

"I must say your mother has some very depressing things to say," remarked Claire to Grandmother Scholar. She was smiling, but Barney could tell she was almost angry. "How could she say a thing like that in front of Barney . . . that his mother died having him. It could really upset him, particularly as he knows that I'm going to have a baby soon."

"She can be so difficult — and unkind," agreed Grandmother Scholar apologetically. "I think she feels it's a sign of weakness to say nice things, and all her memories seem to be bad ones. But what can one do? She's so old— she's eighty-eight— you don't like to be equally unpleasant back to her."

"I'd like to," said Troy, and wandered off to lean against the wall in a forgotten corner of the room.

"Uncle Guy," Tabitha cried, "I want to know something that you know about and I don't — a family thing."

"I'll do my best to answer," Great-Uncle Guy said, giving her an unexpected shy, eager smile.

"Well, we found out by accident that we had another great-uncle — an unknown one (he's in the photograph just tucked in at the side), but we don't know his name or even if he is alive. Can *you* tell me?"

"Well," began Great-Uncle Guy, looking rather helplessly at Claire, "provided you don't mention him in front of your great-grandmother . . ."

"Go slowly so that I can take notes!" commanded Tabitha hopefully and began to feel for her notebook.

But Claire stopped her. "Dear Tabitha," she said. "No notes! I don't want your great-grandmother to think I'm bringing you up with no manners, and I can't help feeling she might be critical of your note-taking." Tabitha sighed, but she obediently let her hand fall and fixed Great-Uncle Guy with her determined stare instead.

"What was his name?" she asked.

"What do you think, Janet?" Great-Uncle Guy asked Grandmother Scholar. "It can't do any harm to . . ."

"Cole!" Grandmother Scholar told Tabitha. "His name was Cole, and he was your Great-Uncle Barnaby's favourite brother."

"Coal?" exclaimed Tabitha. "Coal, like — like what you put on the fire?"

"Cole, like Old King Cole," Grandma Scholar said and Great-Uncle Guy took over.

"He ran away from home when he was very young and he drowned in a river down south. It was years and years ago, and by now it's easy for us to go for a long time without thinking about him at all."

"Perhaps he drowned himself," Tabitha suggested, trying as usual to make life dramatic and alarming.

"Perhaps he did," agreed Great-Uncle Guy, surprisingly. We'll never know. He certainly wasn't a very happy boy — though I don't want to go into just why he wasn't happy, if you don't mind, Tabitha."

"Yes, Tabitha — that's quite enough," said Claire. "You do — you really do — talk far too much."

Tabitha grinned at her grandmother.

"I know I do," she answered. "Everyone's always telling me I do and really and truly, I don't mean to. Today I meant to hide away and be silent like Troy.

23

But there are so many questions and words, someone's got to use them or they might go rusty or get
mould on them or something."

"Claire, I *like* to hear her talk," said Grandma
Scholar, "and I don't get much chance. Come with
me Tabby and help with the afternoon tea and tell me
about your notebook at the same time "

"I'll take Barney," offered Great-Uncle Guy. "If
you can worm your way over here, Barney, there's a
little space behind that chair you can have all to
yourself."

He stalked across the room, tall and yet bent at
the same time, like a heron picking its way over an
estuary. "I'll get some books for you. And do you like
milk with your tea? Or would you rather have orange
juice?"

"Tea please," said Barney because, although he
preferred the taste of orange juice, he liked the warm
feeling that tea gave him inside, and he thought it
would be more grown up and respectful to a dead
great-uncle who had happened to share his name.

"Sugar?" asked Great-Uncle Guy. "Yes — of
course! And I'll bring you a really big slice of your
grandmother's orange cake."

Barney sat in the little space studying the closest
knees. His father and Great-Uncle Alberic were talking to Great-Granny. Beyond them, wrapped in her
own silence, Troy leaned against the wall as close to
the door as she could get, sweeping the room with a
glance so stormy that it was a wonder the flowery
curtains did not billow out wildly and the pictures

fall from hooks under the black magic of her eye. Tabitha and Claire were nowhere to be seen.

When the books came they were all very old ones and all with small print, except for one tall one that was merely a scrapbook filled with post cards, cigarette cards and pictures cut out of long-forgotten magazines. Barney opened one of the thickest books. "In a Canadian Lumber Camp," he read. Opposite this heading were old, muddy-brown photographs. Uncle Guy put a cup of tea and a generous slice of cake beside him.

"I'll be back with you in a moment, Barney," he said, and went off to talk to one of the family friends. For the first time that day Barney felt alone. He watched people vaguely, letting his thoughts go backwards and forwards in their own way.

Sometimes he thought that there was a mountain inside his head with many roads winding up and down around it. His thoughts were like different coloured cars zigzagging backwards and forwards, often unseen and then sometimes showing up on some clear corner. There went his worry about the ghost — there went his happy feeling about home. Sometimes a thought would suddenly appear from a gully or out of a forest and surprise him, because he hadn't known it was there. For example — if your mother died when you were born, did that make you in some way a murderer, even though it was not a thing you could remember or do anything about? And was it very dangerous to have a baby? Barney sighed deeply. Sometimes thoughts seemed to go in little convoys. He did not miss his real mother, which did not seem very kind of him. He wished he could miss her a little bit, but it is hard to miss someone you have never known. If she had stayed alive he would never have had Claire, and he did not believe his real mother could have been nicer than Claire. Barney sat looking at the muddy photographs of a Canadian lumber camp but not really seeing them. Up and down the mountain in his head flashed ideas. They came into sight and then vanished again into caverns, dark forests and around steep corners.

Somehow, without quite knowing how, Barney became aware that his Scholar relations were looking at him. He lifted his eyes from the page and met the dark eyes of Great-Uncle Alberic. He looked away and found his grandfather and Great-Uncle Guy were both studying him too. All three faces wore the curious sharpness he had seen on Great-Granny Scholar's wrinkled face when she had heard of yesterday's faint. Highly embarrassed, Barney put down *The Boy's Annual*, tried to forget his zigzagging uncomfortable thoughts and began to look at the scrapbook instead. As he touched its cover, there began the thin singing drone that had filled his ears yesterday and which began to fill them now. He lifted his head. They were all still watching him and he hated to be watched. Desperately he began to turn the pages, and the drone died away almost entirely, though he knew it was still there really, going on very softly, so that he felt it rather than heard it. He turned yet another page and there before him, flat in this old scrapbook, was the boy in blue velvet, his curls no longer fading into the air like smoke but printed firmly on paper. The mouth was a little open, smiling just as he had smiled yesterday. There was the lace collar, there were the pink fingers. But it was not a ghost any longer, just an old faded picture in an old, faded scrapbook.

"Let's see!" said Tabitha, coming up behind him and standing over him. "Where did you get it?"

Across the top of the page handwriting began to appear— very clear, curly writing, put down by some invisible hand. Barney blinked, but there was no doubt about it. An invisible hand holding an invisible pen was writing a message especially for him, and even before all the words had been set down he knew what it was going to say. "Barnaby's dead! Barnaby's dead, and I'm going to be very lonely." Then the pen drew a speech balloon around the words and pointed them to the mouth of the blue velvet boy. There was no more after that. Barney waited a second or two and then — unwillingly, but needing to know — put out a finger and touched the writing. The ink smudged. It was still wet. Shuddering, he closed the book and pushed it away so fiercely that he upset his tea all over Grandma Scholar's blue carpet.

"Oh, Barney!" wailed Claire coming up from somewhere. "What have you done? Fetch a cloth, Tabitha, quickly."

But Tabitha was staring at Barney with her mouth open

"Did you see?" she cried to Claire. "Did you see what happened? Barney wrote a sort of message in that book without touching it. No pen or anything! Words just came. It was like magic."

"Don't talk to me about magic." Claire was on her knees mopping with her handkerchief. "A cloth! Where's a cloth! Oh, thank you, Janet. I'm so sorry."

"He didn't touch the page. Just looked at it," Tabitha babbled. "I've never seen anything like it except on television." But no one was listening to her except perhaps Great-Uncle Guy and Great-Granny Scholar. Everyone was taking notice of the spilled tea and not Tabitha's declarations of magic.

Barney rescued the books from under Claire's feet and piled them up, the scrapbook on top of the pile. A name written on the cover many years ago was still readable. This writing was dry and faint and childish, but there was something familiar about its curly letters. *Cole Scholar*, Barney read with no surprise at all. He had known what name it would be. The thin drone rushed back into his ear, where it sang for a second and then grew silent, really gone away this time and not just waiting.

"It's well and truly time we went," said Claire, looking up from a discussion about tea stains with Grandma Scholar. Troy wandered away from her wall, and Claire herded Tabitha and Barney before her. They said goodbye to their grandparents and their great-uncles and to their great-granny, deep in her chair, saying nothing, but angry between her eyes and at the corners of her mouth. Just before they left she said unexpectedly to Tabitha, "I heard what you said, and I think you should be old enough by now not to go showing off trying to make yourself interesting by telling silly stories."

"It wasn't a story," Tabitha said, and anyone who knew her could tell that she wasn't showing off this time. She was puzzled and even a little bit frightened. "It was true! I always say what's true, don't I, Troy? It's one of those things that's wrong with me."

"She does tell the truth," agreed Troy. "Better to be like me and tell only lies."

This was a peculiar thing for anyone to say and particularly for silent Troy. Grandmother Scholar did not seem to notice how peculiar it was. She was not listening to Troy. Instead she was looking at Barney — glaring at him almost. Then she turned her black eyes up to Claire and John.

"You'll have to watch this one," she said. "He's one of the unreliable kind. We've had them before and they make a lot of trouble for others."

"What a thing to say!" Claire cried a moment later as they got into the car to go home. "Oh dear! I always want you to behave marvellously in public so people will know what a wonderful stepmother I am. But I don't care if she's one-hundred-and-fifty, she shouldn't speak to a little boy like that — not in front of everyone. You're not unreliable Barney, don't think it, though it was clumsy of you to spill that tea."

"She wasn't talking about the tea, I don't think," said Troy restlessly, and Barney was startled to see in Troy's eyes, under her frowning black brows, a sudden sharpness, like that on Great-Granny Scholar's face, like that he had seen when his grandfather and his great-uncles looked at him, the expression of a cat that has seen the beginning of some movement deep in the shadows.

4

A Crimson Line

"Something's wrong with you," Tabitha said, sliding through Barney's bedroom door. "May I come in?" she added, when she was already safely in and could not be got out again.

"Nothing's wrong," said Barney, pretending to read his book.

"Something is!" Tabitha insisted. "I saw, don't forget. The writing was wet, and there was no pen or ink anywhere around."

"You must have dreamed it," Barney said, still not looking at her, thinking that if he did not see her she might go away.

"No, I didn't!" Tabitha exclaimed indignantly. "I *saw* it — the writing went crawling right across the page like caterpillars. I don't make mistakes — not that sort of mistake. I've only got to close my eyes and I can see it absolutely clearly all over again. Go on Barney — tell me. Please tell me."

Barney squashed himself down into his pillows. "You're being nosy," he mumbled. "You'll just write it all down for your novel."

He did not want to talk about his ghost to Tabitha and then hear her gossiping about it at breakfast tomorrow, giving her own theories and somehow taking it over. It was odd, because the ghost had frightened him — indeed it was still frightening him — but he did not want it to be turned into just another entry in Tabitha's notebook. He would have liked to tell Claire, but he also knew that she was the one person who must not know.

Tabitha sat on the edge of the bed and studied him as if he were a rare species of something.

"I know I'm nosy," she said mildly. "I just can't help it. Secrets are like sore places — I know I should leave them alone but I can't help bothering about them. And if something's wrong I might be able to help . . . I can be very helpful sometimes. Is something wrong?"

Suddenly Barney, looking at Tabitha's round face and shaggy curls, felt that she could be comforting as well as irritating — that he had to tell someone about his ghost, and that Tabitha, who was such a good talker, might turn out to be a good listener, too.

"If I tell you," he said, "do you promise not to tell anyone else, especially Claire?"

"Why not Claire?" asked Tabitha suspiciously. "Have you been doing something wrong? Don't worry if you have! Claire's great. She grumbles a bit but she'd always be on your side — don't you know that?"

"I know she would," agreed Barney. "That's why! I mean that's why not! She'd only worry, and I don't want to worry her. Remember how she used to be about Mantis and Bigbuzz and the others."

"Well, not surprising!" said Tabitha. "Most kids of eight have grown out of those imaginary friends." She looked uncertain. "You're still trying to make out you *didn't* imagine them? I used to think you were awfully good at pretending. I got so that I used to see Mantis myself — almost. I was always *almost* seeing Mantis about the place. Anyway, go on, Barney — do tell me about the writing. I won't tell anyone, not even Claire. Promise!"

"Double promise!"

"Ok. Double promise then. Lock lips! Tie up tongue!"

"I'm being haunted and I don't know why!" Barney burst out. "It's been going on for two days now." And he told her about the boy in blue velvet meeting him on the way home from school and about the picture of the same boy in the old scrapbook. As he told his story he could feel his fear edging around him, but it was eased away by Tabitha's presence and by her sharp interest. He felt lighter and freer, almost ordinary again.

"Hey! Wow!" breathed Tabitha at last. "That's completely weird. Are you sure you're not making it up?"

"You made me tell you and now you don't believe me," Barney said indignantly. "Look — I wouldn't make up something I hate so much, would I?"

"You *did* faint," Tabitha pondered. "That's a sort of proof. You weren't pretending about *that*. What did the ghost say? 'Barnaby's dead! I'm going to be so lonely.' "

"Very lonely," corrected Barney. "And that's what's written in the scrapbook."

"I like so lonely better," complained Tabitha. "If

I were a ghost, that's what I'd say: 'sssoooooooooo lonely' — like that. But listen — there's something *you* don't know. While they were all saying goodbye and worrying about the tea stain on the carpet, I sneaked a quick look at that old scrapbook and I found the page with that picture on it because I wanted to read exactly what it had written." Tabitha paused.

"Did you read it?" Barney asked, to hurry her up.

"Well, it wasn't there. There was the picture all right — that was real — but there wasn't any writing, no smudges, no ink, no anything " She looked at Barney enviously.

"Gosh, I wish it were happening to me," she cried. "It's wasted on you. You're scared of it. And here's me longing for life to be mysterious, and it just goes on day after day being all dull and ordinary. I have to *force* it to be interesting."

"I'd let you have my ghost, if I could," Barney answered. "I don't want it. I want things to stay still for a bit and just be ordinary. I don't get bored."

"Well, I must go and think about this," Tabitha said. "If you have bad dreams you can come and get into bed with me. Don't just lie there suffering." She went to the door, suddenly came back, gave him a clumsy hug and kissed him on the ear and then hurried out shutting the door after her.

Barney looked after her in surprise, thinking how different family kisses were from one another. Tabitha had hugged and kissed him as if she had run out of words and had been practising with some new

34

way of talking to him. Then he began to think about the possibility of having bad dreams, which he had not thought of before. With frightening memories behind him, and dreams waiting on ahead, he felt as if he were besieged and sighed heavily into his pillow. After Claire had come in and read him a story, kissed him good night and turned the light out, he lay in the darkness trying not to think either backwards or forwards. Instead he closed his eyes and tried to make sleep come quickly. It wasn't his usual drowsy drifting but a watchful sentry-duty sort of waiting. A dream might come and refuse to give the password. Then he could drive it away. The darkness behind his eyelids was streaked with lights like dim, slow fireworks going off, and it was impossible to feel sleepy. A face flashed into his mind and was gone again, but he knew the face well. It was the face in a photograph of his mother Dove, which stood on the dressing table in Troy's room. Barney wondered if it was Dove who was haunting him, perhaps angry because he had grown so fond of Claire. However he could not really believe she would mind. She looked too cheerful for that. And anyway, because of the message, he was certain that he was being haunted because Great-Uncle Barnaby had died. Something was being required of him, but he could not think what it might be.

"It's no use bothering about it," he told himself sternly and saw his own words float by, lighting up his shut-eyed darkness with letters of fire.

"Think different!" he commanded his anxious

mind. "Different!" he said aloud, to hear his own determination. It was very convincing and he opened his eyes to clear his head by staring into the real outside darkness. The rockets and the fiery letters vanished. "A circus!" he commanded, and shut his eyes again. No circus came into his head, but something nearly as good, for he found himself remembering a Punch and Judy show he had once seen.

Pink and white curtains flew open and Punch squeaked and waved a stick. Barney made himself remember Judy, the baby, a crocodile and a policeman. His memories began to run out and he was still not asleep. But somehow he could not stop watching the Punch and Judy show. The tiny curtains swept closed and then opened again on another scene — not on a puppet play but on a real place, one that Barney had never seen before. This was not something from his own mind, but something that someone was deliberately showing him. Barney was being haunted again.

It seemed to be not night but early morning between the pink and white curtains. There were hills and dark trees and a road winding towards him. Along the road a solitary figure moved at a steady, dogged pace. He could hear footsteps like the tick of a clock, the beat of a heart, but the face was shadowy and hard to see. Barney could not tell whether the person was a man or a woman, but something about its shoulders and its way of walking reminded him of a shorter, angrier version of Great-Uncle Guy. It stopped and stared out between the curtains.

"So there you are," it said. It was a pleasant, light, husky voice and seemed to come from inside Barney's head and not from outside in his bedroom. It was a man's voice and one he was sure he had not heard before. "I'm on my way, you see. We belong together — you and I."

Barney still could not see the face that belonged to that rustling voice.

"I belong here," he whispered back. "This is where my family is — Dad and Claire and Troy and Tabitha. I belong here."

"You may think you do," the voice replied, "but you'll find that, in the end, there's no place in a family for people like us. It is a discovery we all make. You are taking longer to realize it than I did, that's all."

Barney tried to open his eyes, but they would not open. He was not asleep, but the treacherous lids stayed shut, obeying someone else's wishes.

"You obviously don't realize just what you are yet," the voice said doubtfully. "You are a Scholar magician, don't you understand?"

"I'm a boy," Barney said stubbornly. "Just a boy."

"*I* know," the voice went on. "I can feel you there. I can see you. You're like a line of crimson across the world's rainbow. You're the strongest of us all."

"Who are you?" hissed Barney wildly.

"I'm coming," the voice said, not answering his question, perhaps not even hearing it. "I could be there now, this minute, but I'll travel slowly so that you'll have time to get used to the idea of me. You'll get my messages. I'll share my journey with you."

The figure thrust a hand towards him, not threateningly, but as if it wanted to show him something it held. However, the hand was empty. Barney saw long fingers and a palm lined like a map of some unknown continent. Then the fingers branched like twigs, put out green leaves and blossomed pink and white. From between them flew little scarlet birds, no bigger than bumblebees. The pink and white curtains closed and Barney was free to open his eyes again.

He was frightened, but only in a very tired way. If he got up and scrambled into bed with Tabitha she would ask him questions and talk all night. What he really wanted was to tell Claire and hear her voice, warm and cool at the same time, reassure him that there was nothing to worry about, as she went off to do something about it. But he dared not bother her. He knew that when mothers were expecting babies they should have simple, happy lives and not be alarmed with ideas that their children were haunted or perhaps mad. And though his father was closer and kinder than he had been before he married Claire (in those days he had always seemed to be going to work or coming home from it) he was still somebody Barney was not sure about . . . a jolly man who might turn out to be not very interested in his children in the long run. As it happened, Barney had only a few minutes to think about this, for suddenly he knew that sleep had crept up on him and taken him by surprise

"I must be getting used to ghosts," he thought. "It shows you that you can get used to anything," and a moment later he sank thankfully into a kind of darkness without any dreams to trouble him.

5

The Wild Owl

Tabitha began the next day by watching Barney. Early in the morning she came in and looked at him in bed. At breakfast she sat staring at him as if he might be assailed at any moment by owls and bats and rattling bones. But when the Sunday morning grew really hot, ghosts or no ghosts, she went off to the swimming pool.

"Come with me," she said to Barney, secretly. "I've never heard of ghosts at a swimming pool." Barney would have gone, but Claire looked at him carefully and said that he was not looking very well and that perhaps he should stay at home. She did not mention his Friday fainting, but he knew she was still thinking about it.

"I feel all right," Barney assured her.

"You're rather pale," Claire told him, "and you look as if you're dazzled by something . . . as if you can't see us properly. Are you sure you don't have a headache?"

"I don't," Barney said. "I haven't." But Claire would not let him go to the swimming pool. "I've got to look after you, Barney. You're the only one of you there is."

Barney sat on the verandah drawing dinosaurs. Claire braided her long hair and went to help her husband in the garden. Troy stayed, as she often did, in her room full of books, and said nothing to anyone.

It seemed, at first, as if it were going to be one of those restful, rather boring days devoted to work about the house. Instead it turned out to be a day of visitors. The first visitor was Great-Uncle Guy. Up the Palmers' path he stalked in his heronish way.

"You look very busy," he called to Claire and John as they rose up out of the marigolds with surprised faces and dirty knees. "Don't disturb yourselves."

However, it is impossible not to be disturbed by visitors. You have to make them tea and offer them cakes or, if you don't have any cakes, make them sandwiches. Claire did both, rather anxiously, while she talked to Great-Uncle Guy about gardens and dry weather and what a good summer they were having so far. When Barney heard the sound of the cups and the cake being set out on the table he came in too, and Great-Uncle Guy asked him how he was.

"I'm all right!" Barney said, but he sounded so uneasy and guilty that Claire and his father looked at him in astonishment, and he himself was taken by surprise at his own furtive voice. Perhaps it was this and the sight of the teacups that reminded Claire of yesterday's spilt tea.

"I'm afraid we introduced a note of disorder into your orderly gathering yesterday," she said. "Knocking a cup of tea over seems dreadful when we're in a house with a nice carpet. I hope your mother wasn't too upset."

"Not as upset as the tea was," Great-Uncle Guy said, making a small joke. "And as for our orderly gathering — well I sometimes think, Claire, that our lives have been ruined by too *much* order — we Scholars, I mean. I'm too set in my ways to change now, of course, but I enjoy seeing other people managing well without it."

Barney saw Troy appear like a shadow in the doorway behind Great-Uncle Guy. She stood for a moment like a dark spirit with thin hunched shoulders and then, just as he expected her to come in, she vanished again and he heard her door click shut down the hall.

"My mother wasn't a woman who enjoyed having children," Great-Uncle Guy went on. "She would have preferred to have a set of chessmen, I think. She's still a very good chessplayer, you know, even though she is so advanced in years. She did rather try to turn us into chessmen when we were children and move us all around a board of her own invention. Benjamin — your grandfather, Barney — got away to a considerable extent when he married, and Dove escaped right off the board. But Barnaby, Alberic and I have always moved around her like two bishops and a knight. I always thought of Barnaby as the knight, because he *did* manage to go around corners. Still, I suppose I shouldn't criticize . . . it can't have been easy for her, poor woman, not being very fond of children and having to bring up a family of four."

"Five!" said Barney. He heard the word pop out of his mouth like a cork out of a ginger beer bottle.

"Yes . . . five . . . Cole,' agreed Great-Uncle Guy slowly. "I often forget Cole." Yet Barney felt that Cole had been someone Great-Uncle Guy really wanted to talk about. There was a note of relief or satisfaction in his voice as he said the name. "Cole was like a family on his own . . . a family of one, and wild with it."

"Wild? A wild Scholar?" Mr Palmer sounded amused and unbelieving.

"What happened to the famous family order then?"

"It didn't work with Cole," Great-Uncle Guy said, and though he was talking over Barney's head to Dad and Claire, Barney felt that he was being told a story that had a message in it especially for him. "He and my mother — his mother, too, of course — just never hit it off. They were at war from the hour he was born. My father was very fond of Cole and so was Barnaby. (In fact I think Cole might have been my father's favourite, because, deep down, he liked a naughty boy.) But no one in our family could stand up to my mother — no one even tried, except Cole, and he left home as soon as my father died. Well, of course, shortly after that he was dead, too. It was a terrible year for us one way and another — but it was a long time ago," said Great-Uncle Guy, growing suddenly hurried and shy. "No use dwelling in the past too much, is it?" And then he talked about other things and left soon afterwards filled with Palmer tea and cake.

"What do you suppose brought that on?" Mr

Palmer said in a bewildered voice. "Did he really come to see us or to have another look at Barney. He seemed to be watching him all the time, particularly when he thought we weren't noticing."

"Perhaps he thought Barney didn't look well," said Claire. "I think he looks a bit pale myself, and a doctor would notice things like that. Or maybe it's because you look so much like wicked Uncle Cole, Barney, and he wants to freshen his memories. I wonder if wicked Uncle Cole had yellow eyes like yours, too. You can't tell from the photograph."

"Amber!" Barney said firmly. "My eyes are amber." He liked the sound of the word 'amber' which seemed more mysterious than 'yellow'.

"Golden," his dad assured him. "Don't you worry, Barney — she's just jealous because hers are plain old blue. Yellow, indeed! Now — back to the garden! Barney, you could be useful if you're sure you don't have a headache. Don't stand staring at the cake tin."

"I'm not," said Barney slowly. "I was looking at the milk jug." He followed his father and Claire out into the sunshine again.

"Good lord!" exclaimed his father. "More visitors."

A red car had parked itself outside their gate. Up the path came Grandma and Grandpa Scholar smiling nervously as if they were not quite sure of being welcome.

"We should have telephoned," Grandma Scholar said, "but if Mother had heard us she would have insisted on coming, too, and I thought we'd have a nicer time without her."

"Come in! I'll make a cup of tea," said Claire, sounding a little dismayed.

Out of their own house, away from the black magic of Great-Granny, Grandpa and Grandma Scholar were much less papery, almost jolly at times. Grandma Scholar put her arm around Barney while she talked to Claire, and Grandpa Scholar looked at him as if he were a page of fine print that might be understood on close scrutiny. While he looked at Barney he talked about Great-Uncle Barnaby who was to be buried tomorrow. Like Great-Uncle Guy, Grandpa was in a mood to remember their boyhood together.

"You sound as if you were fond of him," Claire said at last, "and yet as a family, you don't seem close. I mean . . ." She became rather pink. "I *don't* mean that you're not fond of each other, but you seem remote. Oh dear — I'm not putting this very well."

"I expect we do seem remote," Grandfather Scholar agreed. "But you see we only have each other. We have a few acquaintances, but somehow we don't have the gift of making close friends and so we've come to depend on one another rather a lot. Barnaby — well he was very shy but he had a loving heart."

"He was a gentle man," Grandma Scholar said. "We'll miss him terribly. He would have loved to marry and have children I think, and yet at the same time he was so afraid of letting people get close to him "

"We were all afraid," Grandpa Scholar said sadly, "but fortunately for me, Barney, I met your grandmother and she was so bossy and determined I couldn't get away." He smiled at Barney and then at his wife. "And we had Dove, your mother, and she was absolutely set on having children herself, so now we have grandchildren. We're the lucky ones of the Scholar family. Things turned out well for us in spite of everything."

It seemed to Barney that once again some mystery was being discussed but not revealed, that his grandparents were telling him something without letting him know just what it was, expecting him to read between the lines that they could see but he couldn't. There was a secret at the heart of their lives, and it had to do with Great-Uncle Cole and with Great-Uncle Barnaby's death. Some balance had been altered when Great-Uncle Barnaby died and now his grandfather and his great-uncles were beginning to stir, some ancient machinery was starting to turn, and old memories were being invoked. He could see that his father and Claire were puzzled and made uneasy by these Scholarly visitations. Looking at his grandmother he asked, "Did you know Great-Uncle Cole?" and felt again that there was relief and satisfaction in the faces his grandparents turned to him. He had asked a question that they wanted to answer.

"I did know him, just a little — yes!" said Grandma Scholar. "He was a lot like you to look at, Barney, but he was a fierce boy, rather like a young owl or perhaps a hawk."

"Whereas Barney seems to be a peaceful boy." Grandpa Scholar sounded as if he were begging Claire and her husband to agree with him. "Cole was at war with the world — or perhaps it was only *our* world. We never had a chance to be sure."

"Was there something wrong with him?" asked Barney. "It sounds as if he had something wrong with him that no one wants to tell."

"No there was nothing wrong — " began his grandfather doubtfully, but his grandmother cut in very firmly.

"There was absolutely nothing wrong with Cole, except that he had a great imagination and he lived by that, rather than by his mother's rules — and of course, she couldn't stand that. You can probably tell that she was the sort of mother who liked to have everything tame and obedient around her."

There was a knock at the door.

"More visitors!" Mr Palmer said, and could not quite keep his voice from sounding fretful. He went to answer the door and came back into the room so expressionless that Barney knew that he was trying hard not to show astonishment. Behind him came the tall grey figure of Uncle Alberic.

Uncle Alberic looked for a second at Grandpa and Grandma Scholar and turned red and blushing with some secret confusion. Then both he and Grandpa Scholar looked at Barney and away again. It was as if they had both understood something and had agreed that it was not to be mentioned.

"Have some tea," said Claire, looking as if she

might giggle. "I'm afraid we've run out of cake, but I'll just go and make a few more sandwiches." Later when the visitors were gone, she said, half-puzzled, half-laughing, "I don't understand it— three of them in one day. They must have planned it."

"Perhaps, with Barnaby dying, they have decided to keep an eye on the next generation," her husband suggested. "They all seemed very interested in Barney, I thought."

"Well — after all he was the one who was here," Claire said. "I could have called Troy, but she knew they were here and obviously didn't want to show herself. John, I felt they were checking up on me. And what on earth *did* happen to that youngest one — Cole? They seem to want to talk about him, but not to tell you anything, and I don't know whether I'm supposed to ask or what. I mean, we're not much wiser about him, are we?"

But Barney felt that he was wiser. He now felt sure that he was being haunted by the dead boy who had been his great-uncle. He could feel that fierce owl moving through his mind, touching his memories, his ideas, his fears, his happiness. As this wild spirit moved into him, Barney was himself changed, and perhaps this change was what the Scholar family was recognizing and responding to. Like compass needles turning to the north, they were moving to face that powerful ghost. All day its messages had come and displayed themselves before Barney. When he opened his eyes first thing in the morning he had seen through his window, not the rather shaggy Palmer lawn and hedge, but a forest filled with glittering birds and dark red flowers, which had slowly faded to let the usual scene show through and then take over. The blue milk jug on the table had wavered into another shape — a head, covered with tight blue curls and a dull bluish skin, crowned with a chain of gold leaves and berries. Its lips had moved, saying words he could not hear and then had given him a terrifying smile. Once the carpet under his feet had felt like the sand and stones of a beach, and the roar of the sea had filled his ears, while later, leaves from Autumn in another country had brushed and rustled past his ankles. The tick of the clock, once a solemn friendly voice in a quiet room, had begun to echo strangely and sound like footsteps. Someone was walking behind him — a long way off — still hidden in a misty distance but coming closer and closer, holding out a hand lined with the map of another world — a magical world, wise and beautiful perhaps, but not Barney's own.

He was no longer terrified by these messengers and messages. They were no more than ghostly appearances, to be observed like clues in a mystery story. But behind them was the sender of the messages, the dark figure with the shining eyes who had looked at him and spoken so clearly to him last night. Barney was afraid of *him* — not afraid of any unkindness, but of his need and purpose. Somehow, for no reason that he could see, he was part of that need and purpose, and it was the sort of purpose that could change his life in some remarkable way just when it had settled down to being the sort of life that he was enjoying and did not want to change for anything a ghost could offer him. He looked up to find Claire frowning thoughtfully over him, and he felt as he did so, the wild owl look out through his eyes and notice her, too.

.

6

The Power of Cole's Wishes

It wasn't until Tuesday that Tabitha really began to notice a difference in Barney. He came down to breakfast that morning sliding in like a shadow and sitting in his place quiet and composed, neither fretful nor complaining. But for the first time Tabitha saw that what Claire had been saying about Barney was true — he looked sick. "Not sick," Tabitha corrected herself, for she knew something that Claire did not know; Barney looked haunted. His face was clear and pale as if it were beginning to be transparent, but the skin under his eyes was dark, almost bruised. Every now and then something strange happened to his eyes. They seemed caught in a glare of light that no one else could see, flooded with a brightness they could not stand. They took on a glassy shine at these times and Barney seemed to falter all over. Once he stared at his cornflakes as if they were moving around the table, then dipped at them with his spoon quite missing the dish.

Tabitha, that careful observer and future novelist, went back into her bedroom and sat on the edge of the bed feeling troubled. She took a few notes without the usual feelings of pleasure and power, out of habit really, giving herself time to think. She found she was remembering the various ghost stories she

51

had read, and for the first time it occurred to her that being haunted might not be simply exciting and interesting, but actually terrifying. She felt a new respect for Barney, who was trying to keep fear locked in his own head. It was a very brave thing to do, thought Tabitha, and immediately became impatient with him too, because he was doing nothing about it. Ghosts could be beaten. Their secrets could be found out and their power taken from them. They could be exorcized. Trying not to remember those stories she had read in which haunted people died horribly, an expression of mortal terror frozen to their dead faces, Tabitha went back down the hall, scarcely noticing her father (who was shouting because he had lost his car keys) or Troy (who had to get to school earlier than either Tabitha or Barney) trying to cram more books into her pack without squashing her school lunch. Barney was still sitting at the table on his own. Claire was somewhere, probably organizing a car key search. Tabitha drew her chair up close to Barney.

"Hey!" she said, half whispering. "Hey, are you all right?"

Barney turned slowly. His gentle amber eyes, so similar in colour to her own but so much milder in expression, looked back at her, and suddenly there was a brief change — a flash, come and gone before she had time to take it in — a sharpness that was not Barney's, the fierceness of some stranger who had looked out at her for a moment and had then hidden himself again. Immediately Barney clapped his hands over his face and bowed his head

"Don't look at me!" he whispered. "He'll see you." Then he straightened up again and sighed. "He's gone now," he said in a matter-of-fact voice. "He comes and goes really quickly."

"Tell Claire," hissed Tabitha. "You've got to tell Claire." For Claire was a person who could be told, sympathetic but filled with the power grown-ups have and children don't, able to call a doctor, or find an expert on black magic in the telephone book, able to pay a fee to a good witch, or simply, somehow, to work out a way of getting rid of Barney's ghost, through a sort of hardy common sense.

"I can't tell Claire," Barney said calmly. "You know that. I told you why not. It's bad for people having babies to get worried and upset."

"But she's worrying now, you drongo!" said Tabitha. "You should see yourself. You're really starting to *look* haunted, you know . . . sort of yellowish and transparent like cooking oil, and your eyes are funny. Claire probably thinks she's giving you poisoned school lunches or something. She'll be *pleased* to know it's just a ghost and nothing to do with her personally. Look *I'm* going to tell her."

"You double promised!" cried Barney looking at her angrily.

"Tell Dad, then . . ." Tabitha suggested rather more uncertainly, for their father, though he was improving every day, seemed more of a distant relative than Claire did, even though they had known him, in a way, for much longer. "Go on, Barn! Do tell Dad!" She put her hand on Barney's shoulder. At that moment a new sound fell on her ears, quiet but distinct, and she turned quickly, half expecting to find Claire or Troy tiptoeing into the room behind her. There was no one there. Down the hall the shouts and excitement of the car key search was still going on, but the other sound went on too, soft and insinuating, quite unmistakably the sound of footsteps. Barney saw her looking around. His face cleared a little.

"Can you hear them too?" he asked. "It's just me — at least, not me making them. It's Great-Uncle Cole, I think, walking after me. He's coming closer and closer all the time. He must be very close if you can hear him too."

A few steps away from Barney, as Tabitha found by quick experiment, the footsteps could not be heard. By standing close to him and touching him, you could hear them clearly, once you knew what to listen for.

Their father raced through the room.

"They're found," he said. "Thanks." He thought Tabitha had been looking for his car keys, too. "I've got to rush. I'm late." He kissed Tabitha on the cheek and Barney on the top of the head and was gone. Claire walked past them to the kitchen.

"What a fuss!" she said calmly. "They were in the bottom of the laundry basket, can you believe it? He'd put them in the pocket of his shorts and then put the shorts into the washing."

Tabitha and Barney stared at her as if she were a person from another world talking an unknown language, both hearing the footsteps as if they were walking along the footpath, just outside the window.

"Come on you two. Time's getting on," Claire said, going into the kitchen and half closing the door after her.

"Tell Dad!" hissed Tabitha for the third time, and Barney wavered. Then he seemed to stiffen up and shook his head.

"He'll only tell Claire," he said. "He tells her everything. And she'll think that I'm mad or spooky or something." He stood up. "There's nothing I can think of doing about it," he said and left the room.

"*I* must tell someone," thought Tabitha as Claire came back with two school lunchboxes, and she considered breaking her double promise. But just as her mouth was in the act of opening to say "Claire, I've got something to tell you," another idea came into her mind. She could go and visit the Scholar grandparents and consult them about Barney's haunting. They might know what to do about a family ghost. On the other hand, thought Tabitha, Great-Granny Scholar would be there sitting in her armchair like she-who-must-be-obeyed, and Tabitha did not fancy pouring her story into that cold ear. Quietly, almost as if he were a sort of ghost himself, Great-Uncle Guy came into her mind. He had been kind and welcoming when they had paid their Saturday visit, and he would probably be at his office that afternoon. Tabitha thought hard about Great-Uncle Guy as she went to school, with Barney following at her heels like a distracted dog. Some of his school friends called to him, but he merely waved and clung close to Tabitha. "Yes," Tabitha thought, "it would be easy enough to get a bus into town and back again." She had a school concession card for bus travel in her school blazer pocket. On the other hand, it would leave Barney to come home alone after school, prey to any blue velvet ghost that might choose to assail him, let alone any other visions or presences that he might not have told her about. It was unpleasant to think of him going home alone with those footsteps coming after him, perhaps getting faster and faster, and overtaking him as he went past that rather lonely green stretch that marked a corner of the town park. Tabitha found she could easily imagine Barney being whisked off the path, could see a horribly thin but hairy arm coming out of the bushes and pulling him into the shadowy tunnels of the hedge. And then of course he would never be seen again. Tabitha shuddered, astonished to find how precious he was, how much she wanted to look after him. Up until then he had simply been a brother, part of the family furniture, around the house whether she wanted him there or not.

"Why Barney?" she thought. "Is it something that goes with the name?" She could not make any sense of this haunting. It just was, and that was all that could be understood about it.

As it happened Barney's teacher rang Claire during the morning to say that she thought Barney was not very well. She asked Claire if she could come and collect him as he seemed frightened to go home alone.

She understood he had fainted a few days ago. Tabitha saw Claire arrive in a taxi and take Barney away. So Tabitha was free after all to visit Great-Uncle Guy when school was over, and this she did.

Great-Uncle Guy's rooms were with the rooms of a lot of other doctors in Harley House, an old building so studded with brass plates that it looked like a battered general hung with the medals of many successful wars. Tabitha had always imagined Great-Uncle Guy removing worn-out pieces and stitching in new ones. She had been rather disappointed to find that he was a pediatrician and specialized in the sicknesses of children. Now she found it reassuring and felt it was a good omen. He might be the very person who would know how to help Barney. She took the lift to the second floor, followed the signposts and arrived, successful and smiling, in Great-Uncle Guy's waiting room.

There was trouble at once with the cool receptionist, she was so very white and immaculate that she seemed to leave a bright outline of herself in the air after she had moved on, so that you saw her where she was and where she had been at the same time. There was something of science-fiction about this which Tabitha would have liked to take notes on, but she was trying to seem particularly polite. The receptionist was just telling her that Great-Uncle Guy was very busy and that without an appointment she would not be allowed to see him, when a door opened and Great-Uncle Guy himself came out talking to a thin woman who held a baby. He stared at Tabitha as if he did not quite recognize her.

"It's me, Uncle Guy, Tabitha Palmer," she said.

"So it is too," replied Great-Uncle Guy, looking surprised. "What can I do for you, Tabitha Palmer? You don't need professional advice I hope."

"No professional advice — at least I don't *think* so," Tabitha declared. "Family advice really. I need some help over Barney." Great-Uncle Guy's smile vanished and his face grew hidden and watchful before her very eyes. He looked as if he understood everything she had to say to him before she told him anything about it.

"Well, let's see," he said and looked at his appointment book. "Can you wait until four-thirty? I've got a cancellation then and we could talk a little. Here . . ." He gave her some money. "Go down the road and get yourself a milkshake or something. That should make the time pass rather more quickly."

Tabitha thanked him profusely. "I'll take a few notes for my novel," she added, giving the receptionist a triumphant smile. And later, at four-thirty precisely, heavy with milkshake and sandwiches, Tabitha was shown into Great-Uncle Guy's office.

Once she was there it was hard to separate Great-Uncle Guy from Doctor Guy Scholar, pediatrician, and she felt for a moment that it would be impossible to talk about anything as unscientific as a haunting. But when Great-Uncle Guy said, "Now Tabitha — what's this all about? What's wrong with Barney?" there was only one thing she could say.

"He's being haunted," she explained, her hesitations put firmly aside. "Since Great-Uncle Barnaby died he's been haunted, and he thinks it's the ghost of the dead great-uncle — Great-Uncle Cole — that's haunting him." Then she blushed with embarrassment for telling such a tale in such a doctorly room. But Great-Uncle Guy did not frown or look scornfully at her. Indeed, she got the curious impression that he had been expecting and fearing not her tale of ghosts, but another similar story, and was relieved to hear her talk of ghosts and not of something worse.

"Now that's remarkable indeed, Tabitha," he said. "I think you'll have to give me more details. For example — what on earth makes Barney think he's being haunted?"

Tabitha was always pleased to give details, but she decided to give her own theory first — a new theory inspired by a milkshake and three sandwiches.

"I think Barney got it wrong," she cried eagerly. "Suppose it *was* Cole's ghost! Well, now that Great-Uncle Barnaby's dead, he'd be a ghost, too, wouldn't he, and Cole would have company. He wouldn't be lonely, so Barney must have got it back to front."

"Lonely?" Great-Uncle Guy was puzzled. "What do you mean? Who's lonely? You're running ahead of me."

Tabitha realized that she would have to begin at the beginning, so she drew on her experience as someone learning to be a future great novelist and told, very precisely, about Barney's encounter with the blue velvet ghost, about the writing which had

59

crawled so eerily across the scrapbook, the smudging of the wet ink and the total disappearance of the message two minutes later. Put into words the hauntings sounded less impressive than they had seemed when they were shut up in her mind. But Great-Uncle Guy seemed impressed for all that.

"I see," he said. "Yes, I see . . ." and he thought it over for himself for a bit. Then he looked directly at her and spoke in a brisk doctorly voice.

"Of course, Tabitha, there is another explanation for all this you know — always supposing that Barney's not simply inventing it — and that is that Barney is — a very disturbed little boy."

"Barney's not disturbed." Tabitha was affronted. "He's a gentle, quiet sort of boy, really well-behaved, too."

"He could be all those things and still be disturbed, you know," persisted Great-Uncle Guy. "Now just think clearly for a moment, Tabitha. Here's a boy who's never known his own mother, but who does know she died when he was born — *because* he was born in fact. That could make him feel secretly very guilty to start off with. I'm not saying it does, but it could. Now, over the last year there's been a new stepmother in the family and that represents something that many children find — well — challenging to adjust to."

"Claire — but Claire's terrific." Tabitha shook her head. "Barney really loves her. You can easily tell that."

"Oh, I'm sure he does," Great-Uncle Guy

agreed. "But don't you see that could make it worse? I mean — now she's expecting a baby herself and Barney knows that having a baby caused his own mother's death. Don't you think he might get so filled up with fears that after a while the fears begin to seem like ghosts to him, things he mustn't talk about, but which are still there, stalking around in his mind. And then, when Barnaby died, the two things — the fear of Claire's death and Barnaby's actual death — became linked together. It could happen like that, you know."

Tabitha saw that it could be like that and also saw the ghost vanishing away into the world of grown-up explanation and theory.

"I suppose so," she agreed doubtfully. "He did make me double promise not to tell Claire and said that mothers expecting babies shouldn't be worried or upset. Well, Dad told us that when Claire first knew about the baby — but . . ." She sat up straighter. "It can't be just that. See — if you stand by Barney and you touch him you can hear the ghost's footsteps yourself. I did this morning, though I'm sure I couldn't hear them last night, and Barney says it's because Cole is getting closer and closer. And that's another thing! If he's getting closer where's he getting closer *from*? That's what I wonder!"

"The ghost's footsteps?" Uncle Guy turned Tabitha's words into a question.

"It's a steady, smudgy sort of walking sound." Tabitha waved her hands in the air. "Not stealthy — I wouldn't say stealthy, exactly — too determined to be stealthy! And also I got the funniest idea this morn ing . . ." She looked at Great-Uncle Guy apologetically. "It sounds mad but I've got to say it. I thought the ghost was not just *following* Barney but was actually *inside* him, too. You see every now and then Barney gets a sort of dazzled look on his face. Once, when I was looking right at him, his eyes went really different, not dazzled but fierce. It was just as if someone else was using Barney's eyes to look at me."

This, then, was what Great-Uncle Guy had been afraid she might tell him. There was a new tightness about his expression, and his expression suggested he was remembering old and troubling things. When he spoke it was as if he were reassuring himself as well as Tabitha.

"It may be nothing," he murmured. "Just troubles hidden away, yet making themselves known in odd ways. That sort of thing does happen after all." Tabitha had to ask a question and she felt that, if she asked it, Uncle Guy would reply by telling her a truth there could be no hiding from.

"Uncle Guy, truly — really and truly — do you believe that Barney has invented a ghost because he's upset over Claire and babies and death and things?"

Great-Uncle Guy decided something inside himself. She could see him do it.

"Tabitha Palmer, truly — really and truly — " he replied, smiling a little, "I don't believe it, and I don't believe he is haunted either. I think Barney is changing, like a caterpillar in its chrysalis. I think he's becoming a different sort of boy, and it's to do with his being a member of the Scholar family. There now."

"Becoming different? How different?" Tabitha cried incredulously.

"I think he's becoming a Scholar magician," said Great-Uncle Guy. "Tabitha, there have always been people in our family — we call them Scholar magicians — who have powers and peculiarities most people just don't have, and it has nearly always brought misfortune on them and on those around them. It's like a family curse. That was the trouble with Cole, you see. That's why we were never to talk about him, or even think about him. I believe Barney may be another of the same kind."

The room shivered with its own silence while Tabitha and Great-Uncle Guy stared at each other. It was Great-Uncle Guy's turn to blush slowly.

"It's true!" he said. "We've got — well, we used to have — letters and diaries going back many years. There used to be a family tree with the magicians marked in red. The curse may well be living on in Barney."

"Is it very awful?" breathed Tabitha. "Is it like being a vampire or something?"

"Nothing like that. At least I don't think so — not really. You see Cole is the only Scholar magician I've ever known. Mind you he certainly could be terrifying. He wasn't happy, of course, but that could have been mainly because of my mother. Dear me, it's hard to say what he could have been like if she had been a little bit less . . . But it's no use guessing

about that. She felt very bitterly about Cole, you see
— very bitterly indeed. The whole thing not only
killed Cole but it ruined my mother. I'd better tell
you — better explain. You should be told anyway.
It's just that we've all been brought up to regard it as a
guilty secret, and it's always been easier just to be
silent.

"My parents — your great-grandparents — were
second cousins. Did you know that? I don't think my
father ever worried about our family being different
with their magic powers but my mother was obsessed
with it. When we were small — Alberic, Benjamin,
Barnaby and I — she used to talk about it continually
and say how glad she was that we were free of it. The
magic thing. Although it could have come to us from
both sides of the family, she told us it only affected
boys. I said the other day to someone that my mother
didn't enjoy having children, but she did love us
older boys, I'm sure of that. However, anytime we
showed any oddness — any individuality, I suppose
you might say — she felt she had to suspect it and
attack it, too. She clipped and pruned us as if we were
a family of standard roses; in the end our lives were all
straight lines. I don't think any of us minded, except
perhaps Barnaby sometimes. He liked to keep things
secret, Barnaby did, particularly from my mother
who needed to know everything. All the same, things
were going quite well for us — but then when I was
nineteen Cole was born."

"Did you know straight away that he was a magician?" asked Tabitha, and her hand wandered long-

ingly towards her notebook. She forced it to come back and lie politely on her knee.

"We knew at once. My mother knew *before* he was born, I think. He was such a fierce, self-willed baby. He began by moving things around. He'd lie there in his cot all tucked in tightly, but the power of his wishes stretched out into the house like — like the tentacles of an octopus. He learned to bring things to him — his bottle, his rattle, anything he happened to want. We would be reading or working and we'd hear him call us — not by crying, simply a voice in our heads speaking our names. Barnaby always went, but my mother would never go unless he cried like a normal baby. She pretended the voice in her head just didn't exist. Once he realized that, Cole refused to cry. For years he refused to talk. As he grew up, he and my mother moved around each other like two adversaries, each looking for a chance to defeat the other — circling, circling, and always in silence. The struggle between them affected us all. In some way it bound us — the four older brothers — together in a sort of unspoken pact of self-defence. We tried not to take sides, although I think that, unknown to me at any rate, Barnaby helped Cole — gave him some sort of attention and love as he grew up. They used to spend time together and Barnaby gave him toys — that scrapbook was a gift from Barnaby. But he gave his presents secretly, because if my mother had found out she would have found some way to prevent it. She hoped to bring Cole into line with the rest of us, you see. She said she knew that he could give up being a magician if he set his mind to it and that it was only a sort of wicked stubborness that made him cling to his powers. He lived like some sort of a wild animal in our house, hiding away, never appearing at mealtimes like the rest of us, never going to school. Most people thought he was some sort of idiot, unteachable, and my mother let them believe this."

"It must have been terrible," Tabitha said, thinking of her own family with thankfulness.

"My mother was sure that her will would win through. She had never lost a battle before, and to begin with I'm sure she really wanted what she thought would be best for Cole. But, as time went by and he remained free and undefeated, she grew afraid, and of all things fear was the one thing she was least fitted to bear. She began to punish Cole cruelly. She began to hate him, and a house of hate slowly destroys the people who live in it. We were all being eaten away by the contest and yet we couldn't leave because, though Cole was free in a dreadful sense, the rest of us were still very much under our mother's thumb. She wanted us there, perhaps to help her win, but mostly to see her triumph. She wanted to conquer Cole and to have her conquest seen and, I suppose, applauded."

It was as if Great-Uncle Guy were telling himself this story. His voice seemed like the voice of someone arguing with himself, and he did not look at Tabitha while he spoke.

"As for Cole, his powers grew and grew. Sometimes he played with us a little, magical game . . .

you'd go in for dinner and find a table fifteen-feet long covered with roasted peacocks and sucking pigs, toppling jellies, trifles, boar's heads, puddings, and pancakes burning in brandy — all a sort of joke. Or you'd be having a bath and suddenly you'd be swimming in clear, warm water by some tropical island, with palm trees and great butterflies and beaches of white sand. It was just as if Cole were offering us presents. Well I would never accept them, I'd refuse to look. I was too much of a chessman, a standard rose. But Barnaby might have. I'll never know now. Anyway, we could all feel Cole's power running through the house like a sort of electricity — a sort of invisible fire. Then, when Cole was about twelve years old my father died. Well, we were all in the front room at home about to go out to the cars — for it was quite a big funeral — when suddenly Cole was among us. For the first time I heard him speak — a light husky voice, really very sweet, as if he might sing beautifully. He was perfectly dressed, behaved admirably, indeed I think the rest of us might have seemed awkward in comparison we were so taken aback. Whenever I'd seen Cole, and that wasn't very often, he was more like a savage, a tribe of one, hunting in and out of our house. 'So Mother's won after all,' Alberic said to me, and my mother did have a look of secret triumph about her. But the next day Cole was gone. We could feel that the house was quite empty. No more electricity running through its walls. Some time later the body of a boy was found in a river down south and mother identified him as Cole

— my magician brother. So he was gone and we, none of us, felt the electricity of the Scholar magicians again until — well, until the other day when you came to visit us and there it was again, beginning in Barney. It was very faint — it was different in many ways — but we couldn't be mistaken, your grandfather, Alberic and I. We knew it all too well. It was like hearing a well-known voice speak from very far away, saying 'Remember me?' "

Both Tabitha and Great-Uncle Guy sat silently, turning their thoughts over for a moment or two.

"Perhaps there are ways of saving someone from being a magician," Tabitha suggested. "Perhaps those old diaries and letters you talked about . . ."

Great-Uncle Guy shook his head.

"No use!" he said. "When Cole left home my mother burned all the old papers, every last letter. And I'm sure that before she did that she had read them through and through, looking for any clue they might have had in them which would have helped her win a victory over Cole."

"But Barney's not like Cole. He *wants* to be ordinary. He said so," Tabitha pointed out. Then she added, "It still could be just what *he* thinks it is — he might be haunted by Great-Uncle Cole's ghost. It could be that."

"No, it couldn't," said Great-Uncle Guy abruptly. "It couldn't . . ." He stood up and walked over to his window, ". . . because after all Cole is not dead. He isn't a ghost."

"Not dead! But you said he was drowned,"

Tabitha cried, standing up.

"My mother must have made a mistake," Great-Uncle Guy replied. "Alberic and I have been tidying up Barnaby's apartment, going through his papers, and we found some letters from Cole — only about two or three, but the last one was dated quite recently. No address. Not that Cole needs to write. I imagine it was just that Barnaby might have enjoyed getting letters from time to time. But it seems Cole is still alive. It's been quite a shock to us."

Tabitha felt she might be turning pale. She wished she had a looking glass so that she could actually see it happening. But almost immediately she thought she could understand what was going on.

"Well, that's what it means, then," she declared. " 'Barnaby's dead. I'm going to be very lonely.' Cole is choosing another Barnaby in the family to be his friend. I'll bet it is Cole all the time sending messages to my brother, trying to get hold of him, now Great-Uncle Barnaby's dead. I don't believe our Barney's turning into a magician."

"I suppose that's possible," said Great-Uncle Guy with a sigh. "I suppose it's possible, but who can tell?"

"We've just got to go on staring at each other with a wild surmise," Tabitha said, quoting with satisfaction a line from a poem in a school collection. "But I'll bet I'm right. Being a novelist has given me a sort of instinct."

"Being a Scholar has given me an instinct, too," said Great-Uncle Guy, rather grimly, but smiling at

Tabitha. "You'd better go home now, Tabitha. It's getting late and I still have work to do. And later on this evening, if I can, I think I shall come and have a word with your parents."

"They'll think you're mad," said Tabitha. "I don't, but they will."

"I have always hated the thought that people might think I was mad," said Great-Uncle Guy, "but I don't know that it matters much anymore."

7

A Telephone Call for Barney

"Where's Barney?" demanded Tabitha coming into the kitchen, her face pink with excitement and importance.

"You're late, Tabitha!" Claire said accusingly. She was looking rather hot and irritable, but that could have been because she was chopping up onions. Onions can have a very bad effect on the temper.

"Sorry!" said Tabitha. "I didn't think you'd mind. I got into one of those talks that go on and on . . ."

"For two hours? Nearly three?" Claire began to look derisive, not easy-going as she usually was.

"Well, I was giving my opinion. You know how I love that." Tabitha leaned against the kitchen door. "Where's Barney? How is he?"

Claire put down her onion knife.

"Oh, I'll take a break," she said impatiently. "Wretched vegetables! It's a pity they make other things taste so delicious. Listen, Tabitha — have you got any idea what's wrong with Barney?"

Tabitha crossed her fingers behind her back.

"No," she said. " 'Flu or something? Well, you know, he's always quiet. I'm always noisy, and Troy and Barney —"

"Yes, I know all that," Claire interrupted her.

"There are different ways of being quiet, and Barney's quietness used to be a happy one, and now for some reason he isn't happy any more. He's always been such an affectionate boy and suddenly he doesn't want to be touched or hugged or even to walk beside me. However, the doctor says he can't find anything wrong with him. He thought he might have migraine headache because his eyes look strained but Barney says, 'No headache!' and I suppose he's the one to know. Anyway now he's got a bottle of vitamin pills to take — vitamin pills, for goodness' sake!"

"Where is he?" asked Tabitha for the third time.

"He's in his room lying on his bed — not reading or drawing or anything — just lying and listening."

"Listening?" Tabitha asked cautiously.

"Well, not really listening, of course, because there's nothing to listen to. He just looks as if he's listening."

"I'll go and see him," Tabitha cried. "I'll see if he will tell me if anything's wrong. He might be in trouble at school."

"His teacher didn't say anything about any trouble," said Claire dubiously, returning to the attack on the onions.

Barney was just as Claire had described him, lying on his bed listening. He was so waxy and still that for a moment Tabitha wondered fearfully if he were dead, but then he opened his eyes and looked at her, vaguely. As she came up close to his bed and touched him a pulse began to beat in the air around him and she could hear what he had been hearing all the time — the footsteps coming closer and closer from some mysterious country that might not even be part of the world. Tabitha looked around the room. Evening sunshine was still touching the walls and the whole room was filled with a pinky gold light. There were Barney's planes, there were his books, all quite as usual, but over them, through them, stalked the footsteps, padding steadily on. They made her angry.

"I don't know how you can just lie there doing nothing," she said.

"What can I do?" asked Barney in a voice that was both tired and irritable. "I can't do anything about the air around me, can I? You can't spray footsteps as if they were flies."

"You could try to find out what it means," said Tabitha. "It's because of something, you know."

"Yes, but not because of anything I've done," objected Barney. "It's because of things that happened before I was even born, I think. Look — suppose it's because I'm the youngest in the family — Well, I can't just decide to be the eldest, can I?"

"You can ask and find out things," Tabitha declared. "That's what I've been doing for you. For instance I talked to Great-Uncle Guy this afternoon."

Barney actually sat up.

"Did you really?" he asked accusingly. "Did you really tell him about me?"

Tabitha couldn't help feeling a little guilty, but not very much.

"I didn't promise not to tell Great-Uncle Guy," she said, "and I'm glad I did because he had a lot that was interesting to say. I'm not like you! I've got to know what's going on."

Barney looked at Tabitha as if she were a specimen of some species entirely different from his own and wondered how he could explain to her that at present the footsteps were filling his mind like the constant beating of a drum, leaving very little thought or feeling to use up on curiosity, or even for worry about Claire. How could he really explain that continually, through the familiar world, he caught glimpses of places he had never seen before in his life, things he did not recognize . . . a little, green, rounded hill so freckled with sheep that it looked as if it were covered in big daisies; a stormy coastline where waves crashing on the rocks sent up great swirls of salt water and foam, briefly embroidering the grey air with lace and pearls. Only ten minutes ago he had been shown a stretch of mud left by an outgoing tide now crossed with dark lines — the tracks of large animals, perhaps horses. It seemed that the lines were spelling out words, as if the animals had written down the story of their wanderings, but it was not a story that Barney could read. He had scowled at the scene before it faded as mysteriously as it had come. These little pictures, coming and going without warning, were things that someone else was seeing — the someone whose footsteps sounded through Barney into the quiet of his little room. They were given to Barney as presents, as promises, for the person who was seeing these things thought they were beautiful and wanted to share them with someone.

But Tabitha was in full cry, gabbling out the details of her visit to Great-Uncle Guy and telling him about the Scholar magicians. Family curses, burned letters, great-grandmother's determination turning into a sort of wickedness, a drowned boy. Old happenings tumbled off Tabitha's busy tongue as she leaned towards Barney, her face bright with interest. She explained about Great-Uncle Cole, the magician child, born to a woman who, for some reason or other, hated magic. But all the time she was talking, Barney could tell Tabitha was saving something until last. She kept the important, excited look of a person swollen out with secrets. Now, at last, she was going to tell him, astound him with a revelation.

"And *then* . . ." Tabitha paused dramatically. "*Then* he said — are you listening Barn, because this is incredible — that they had been sorting through Great-Uncle Barnaby's papers . . "

"I thought you said the papers were all burned," protested Barney.

"No — not those papers, other papers. Great-Uncle Barnaby's income tax and parking tickets and all that sort of thing, I suppose. Anyway they were looking through them and they found actual *letters* from Great-Uncle Cole. He'd been writing to Great-Uncle Barnaby. You see? He isn't dead. He isn't a ghost and you're not being haunted. It's all something else."

"Letters! Cole doesn't need to send letters," cried Barney.

Tabitha suddenly lay back in her chair.

"That's what Great-Uncle Guy said. He thought that Great-Uncle Barnaby probably liked to *get* letters. But aren't you surprised?" Tabitha gave Barney a hopeful smile.

"I already knew he couldn't be dead," Barney answered. "At first, I thought he was, because everybody said so. But he just feels so alive that I began to think he couldn't be dead. Anyhow, it *is* him though, whatever he is, and he's moving from place to place towards me, sending his thoughts on in front of him. Ok it's not a ghost — more a sort of shadow coming nearer and nearer across the world."

"What's he like?" asked Tabitha.

"Very shadowy," Barney answered. "He can be any shape, I think, but I know the palms of his hand and his owl eyes and I know his voice. I'll always know him. It's more like tasting a flavour than recognizing a face."

Tabitha flung herself down on the end of Barney's bed in a sort of writhing fury of impatience. "What does it mean?" she cried. "Things have got to have meaning."

"I told you," Barney said. "He's lonely. He wants me to be friends with him."

"But that can't be all," Tabitha snapped. "Gosh, if that's all, well, *be* friends with him and let's forget it. *Be* friends with him and don't make yourself sick."

"He's too weird and spooky," whispered Barney, shivering. "It's like blackness — or a cave suddenly wanting to be friends with you. That's what it feels like. Like a cave waiting for you, and you might have to go into it and not come out again."

Tabitha sat up. She made up her mind to try a new direction of attack.

"Troy!" she said. "We could ask Troy. She remembers our mother and the Scholars in the old days. She had that photograph. Troy might know something useful."

"She wouldn't know more than Great-Uncle Guy," Barney objected. "And he couldn't do anything. He didn't tell you how to stop the footsteps did he?"

"He said he'd keep in touch," said Tabitha, leaping to her feet. "But then *he* doesn't believe you're being followed or haunted. He's got his own theory — that you're turning into a Scholar magician because you filled grandpa's house with electricity on Saturday. Come on, let's ask Troy. She's probably in her room now."

Barney rose and followed Tabitha in a resigned way, knowing she would not let him alone until they had tried out her new plan. They went down the hall to the door at its very end — Troy's room. Tabitha did not bother to knock. She just pushed the door open and, with Barney shuffling half unwillingly after her, barged into Troy's solitude.

Barney and Tabitha were both untidy, and even when everything had been picked up and their bed-covers straightened, their rooms still looked as if they had been disordered a few minutes ago and would be disordered again ten minutes later. Neatness had not been welcomed there. Troy's room, on the other hand, was always tidy. Troy was the one who picked up, folded, straightened, and brushed down — everyone in the family knew that. Yet today there was something about Troy's tidiness, even when it was expected, that was shocking — something eerie and astonishing. The books in her bookcase were in exact order of size, pulled out to the very edge of the shelf and not a quarter of an inch forward or back. Her bed quilt was perfectly flat, its corners done like the corners of a hospital bed. Troy's homework was set out on her desk as immaculately as if she had been going to do a heart operation on it. Her tiny writing ran across sheets and sheets of paper as if a regiment of minute insects with inky feet had marched with enormous precision over the pages. The smallness and tidiness of that writing made Tabitha uneasy though she couldn't think why. Neatness was well known for being a good thing, so why did Troy's neat room look somehow so mad — so demented?

In the middle of the room stood Troy herself, the only untidy thing in it. She turned to meet them, her pale face looking out of its cloud of dark hair like a ghost glimpsed at the top window of a dark tower.

"Hello!" she said abruptly. "What do you want?"

The muffled tread of the footsteps seemed suddenly louder here. Barney gazed around him in distraction. Tabitha looked at him and frowned, irritated by his vagueness just when she needed support. She could not know that he was being shown a cloud of small steel-blue butterflies rising from a clump of meadow grasses and wild flowers.

Tabitha turned to Troy again.

"It's Barney!" she said "He's being haunted — well not exactly haunted, more sort of followed."

It was the second time that day she had told the story and her voice had a feebleness about it that dismayed her, but it was partly because Troy's face had been so unexpectedly wild, the face of a person struggling with pain or doubt. Even now, while it was ironing itself out, becoming the still, inexpressive face that Troy usually wore, the slant of eyebrows, the tightness of her long mouth, suggested that Troy was struggling with some ghost of her own.

"What's wrong?" Tabitha asked. "You look all hot and bothered."

"Nothing's wrong. Just homework." said Troy shortly. "You know!"

Tabitha looked over at the neat pages set out on Troy's desk.

"Anyhow, what's this about Barney being haunted?" Troy looked at Barney. "He looks ok to me."

Tabitha went on with the story again, wishing Barney would speak for himself, would do something to show Troy how serious it all was. But Barney said nothing, just looked around at the butterflies no one else could see.

"Well, it all sounds pretty strange to me," said Troy at last. "Are you sure you're not making it up?"

"Of course not," Tabitha said. "Can't you hear the footsteps yourself?" She took Troy's hand and placed it on Barney's shoulder. The footsteps seemed suffocatingly close. They filled the room, stalking through its stillness, changing nothing, but sounding as if they would follow, follow to the end of the world.

"There," breathed Tabitha, alarmed by them all over again.

Troy's face was a mask, neither anxious nor scornful.

"I don't hear anything," she said. "Why should I? There's nothing to hear."

Even Barney reacted. Like Tabitha, he stared disbelievingly at Troy, his mouth a little open with surprise.

"But you *must* hear them!" exclaimed Tabitha at last. "They're so loud now. Anyone could hear them. Stand here where I'm standing now."

Troy grudgingly moved forward a step or two.

"I still don't hear them," she said, shrugging her bony shoulders. "Is it a sort of game you're playing? I'm not in the mood to play."

Tabitha could not credit it.

"Gosh — perhaps I'm being haunted too," she cried. "I thought it was only Barney, but perhaps it's rubbing off on me as well. Now Troy — listen again. I can hear them perfectly clearly. Are you sure you can't hear even one footstep?"

"There's nothing to hear," Troy replied stubbornly.

"I told you," Barney said to Tabitha. "That's two people you've told, and it hasn't helped. There's nothing to be done except . . ."

Somewhere in the air around him he felt a silent storm of change. The balance of the last two days was about to alter. Something new was rushing at him faster than he could understand.

"There's nothing to do except *wait*!" he shouted desperately. "Just wait, that's all!" He shouted the last words at Tabitha and as he did so the footsteps stopped.

The room was quiet except for an echo from the ceiling that said, "Wait!" back to him and then fell silent, too.

"They've stopped," said Tabitha. "They *have* stopped, haven't they, Barney?" Barney nodded. The silence fell again.

It was broken by the shrill cry of the telephone in the hall.

None of them moved, and at last Claire had to come through from the kitchen to answer it.

"It's for you, Barney," she called.

Barney stood still.

"Go on!" Troy jerked her head at the door. "Phone! Go on, Barney. It's for you."

"I don't want it," said Barney.

"Barney!" called Claire impatiently.

Slowly Barney walked down the hall. The hand that lifted the receiver was heavy with reluctance. Claire stood in the doorway looking back at him with the sort of curiosity parents feel when a strange voice asks for one of their children.

"Hello," he said in a small voice.

The phone sighed.

"Barnaby?" it asked, in the familiar, husky voice of his shadowy ghost.

"Barney! I'm called Barney!" Barney hissed.

"I've arrived," the voice said. "I'm here in your town."

"I know," Barney answered. Behind him he knew Claire was listening.

"I could be with you now," said the voice, "but I thought you might need time to get used to the idea of me. I can tell you are finding this all very strange."

Barney said nothing.

"Are you there, Barney?" asked the voice. "Can you hear me? Can you hear me?"

"You've got the wrong one," Barney cried at last. "It's not me you're looking for. It's a mistake."

"I don't think so," said the voice "I'm sure you are the one. But you don't know it yourself yet. We don't always know what we are in the beginning."

"I *do* know," Barney said desperately. "I know now. I'm not! It's not me!"

There was a soft laugh over the phone.

"You'll find out," the voice said. "See you soon."

"*Who* on earth was that?" Claire asked.

"No one much!" Barney said turning his back on her. "Just someone from school playing a game."

He went wearily down the hall, pushing past Tabitha into his own room. Then he shut the door.

8

Melting with Fear

Claire had made a particularly delicious dinner that night, but her family ate it in silence. Tabitha for once was bewildered into thoughts she did not want to talk about. Troy, frowning, ate her meal in an absentminded way. Barney had nothing to say. Claire, glancing from one to the other of them, grew very quiet and ate almost unwillingly. Mr Palmer sat down in a good humour, but as he got only short answers to his questions, and no reply to his comments, he stopped talking too, eating with a puzzled watchfulness like someone in difficult and even hostile company. Then, without any warning, Claire dropped her knife and fork, put her face in her hands and began to cry.

"Darling!" said her husband, putting his hand out to her and getting his sleeve in the gravy. "Claire — dearest pet, what's wrong?"

"Nothing!" wailed Claire like a miserable child. "Nothing! Well — nothing much." Then she cried again. "I feel such a failure," she said. "I always mean — always mean to be good-tempered, but get snappy and cross about things. And now I feel such a failure. There's Troy looking as if she's — I don't know — she looks as if she's tearing herself to bits inside. And Barney looks like a ghost — I know something's gone

83

wrong for him and he won't tell me what it is."

"I'm all right!" said Tabitha anxiously.

"Well — even you're quiet tonight," Claire said, and giggled through her tears. "Sometimes I just long for you to shut up, and then, when you do, I'm sure it must be because there's something wrong."

Mr Palmer looked at his children.

"It's hard for a father to know," he said. "I've been away at work all day. *Is* anything wrong?"

Barney looked at Tabitha.

"I told you so," Tabitha couldn't help saying, but it was Troy who really answered.

"Nothing that is anyone's fault," she said. "It's honestly nothing to do with you, Claire — at least part of it is, but only in a way. For instance Barney's frightened about the new baby coming. He thinks if he upsets you you might die having it, because our mother did. You and Dad have tried so hard not to make a big thing of it so as *not* to worry him, that you probably haven't explained enough. I don't think anyone's told him that Dove had a weak heart, but that Claire's got a heart like an ox."

"Thank you!" said Claire, laughing and crying at the same time. "Oh dear — my nose is dripping and I haven't got a handkerchief. Hang on a moment."

"It would ruin your lovely dinner to have your nose dripping all over it," agreed Tabitha. "Hurry up, Claire."

She was, however, staring at Troy, wondering how Troy had known about Barney's anxiety for Claire without being told, while she, a future great novelist, had had to ask questions to find out. Barney stared, too, at Troy as if she had performed a magic trick before his very eyes. Brought out almost accidentally at dinner like this, his fear for Claire seemed immediately much smaller and more manageable. Troy gave him a little, flickering smile, partly guilty, perhaps because she had given away something that she knew he had wanted kept secret.

"True or false, Barney?" asked his father.

"True," mumbled Barney.

Troy had not finished yet.

"It was really harder for Barney than for Tabitha and me before you married Claire," she said. "Mrs Gaines liked girls, but she just didn't like little boys, so she wasn't terribly nice to him. Not cruel or anything, just not interested or affectionate." (Mrs Gaines had taken care of the Palmer children after school in the days before Claire.)

"She *said* she didn't like boys," Tabitha reported. "She kept on saying boys were a lot of trouble, because her own boys were a lot of trouble, and she didn't seem to notice that Barney wasn't any trouble at all. It was just as if she put her own home boy-trouble on to Barney without him doing anything to deserve it."

"And neither of you thought of mentioning this to me," her father said rather angrily.

"Well," said Troy, "be your age, Dad! What would you have done? Would you really have looked around for someone else? Mrs Gaines was so convenient, just down the road and very reliable and she didn't charge very much. Besides a lot of the time you were so miserable yourself . . . . There's just no point in telling everything you know unless its going to *change* something. You've just got to put up with what can't be helped. We all do. You did. I do. So does Barney. The way things are is the way things are."

It was her father's turn to stare at Troy in the alarmed fashion of someone whose secret has been revealed. "You seem to know a lot," he said uneasily. Troy did not laugh. Barney could never remember hearing her laugh, but she gave one of her rare smiles.

She held out her hand palm upwards.

"Cross the gypsy's palm with silver," she said. "I've had to live with you lot, day after day after day. I can't help knowing things."

But her father still continued to look at her uneasily.

Claire came back into the room. She had not only blown her nose. She had washed her face as well and looked almost back to normal except for her pink eyes.

"All better!" she said. "Oh dear! Why does crying always make you feel so silly? I don't think it should, really."

"Claire, dear, everybody loves you," her husband told her rather awkwardly, and then fell silent.

"You see I was right!" Tabitha turned to Barney. "I told you you'd worry her more not telling. I don't agree with what Troy said — you should always tell everything. That's why I'm going to be a novelist

— so that I can tell."

"People who tell everything end up by having nothing to tell," Troy observed crushingly.

"Ha! Ha! Very clever!" Tabitha cried cheerfully. "Anyway, what about you, since we're on the subject of telling. You go around frowning to yourself and shut yourself up in your room and mostly don't have anything to say. It's like living in the same house with a secret agent. So there!"

"I *like* frowning," replied Troy. "I save my smiles as rare treats for my friends."

"What friends?" asked Tabitha. "You haven't got any."

"My family," Troy replied. "You and Barney and Claire and Dad. Also I have a lot of homework to do in case you haven't noticed. I've got exams to pass — real exams, not those rubbishy primary school exams which everyone passes, one way or another." And she began to eat the last of her dinner in a way that said, 'No more questions.'

"Claire," Tabitha went on. "I promise I won't argue over the dishes tonight. It's not my turn to wash but if you try to make out it is, I'll just smile in a saintly way and do them. Maybe tomorrow, too! But I can't promise for the day after that. I'll probably be back to normal by then. I can't keep up niceness too long at a time."

"Tabitha — you're very kind," Claire said. "Oh dear! What an idiot — not you, me!"

"Barney and I will do the dishes tonight," Mr Palmer said. "I think we owe ourselves some time alone together and if we've got to do the dishes to get it, well, that's part of the price we must pay."

"I'll help," cried Tabitha, suddenly curious, but her father smiled at her and shook his head. "Ok do your old dishes and see if I care. I've got some really important things to do and I'm going to do them — so there!"

It was very restful in the kitchen. Mr Palmer turned out to be a very good dishwasher, rinsing each dish carefully and then filling the sink with clean, hot water and sparkling bubbles. Even the saucepans, the villains of washing-up time, looked orderly and easy as they waited on the stove.

In the soft, slightly steamy air of the kitchen it was easy to talk about Claire and the new baby, easy to listen to his father talk about Barney's dead mother.

"She had a fault in her heart," Mr Palmer said, "and the doctor told her it would always be risky for her to have children. However, she was very determined. Well, we had Troy, and I thought 'We've been lucky.' One's enough! And then we had Tabitha, and I thought that made a nice family. But Dove loved babies and children. 'Just one more little one,' she said. 'A boy this time!' Poor Dove — she pushed her luck a bit too far, her silly heart gave up on her and she died."

"Did she know it was *me* being born?" asked Barney greedily. "Did she know I was a boy?"

"I don't know. I hope so," said his father sadly. "She always talked as if you were a boy, and she always seemed to have known that Troy and Tabitha were going to be girls. It wouldn't have made any difference. She'd have loved you either way, boy or girl. And now Claire loves you — and Claire — well, as Troy said, Claire's as strong as an ox. We're lucky again Barney, and there's nothing to worry about."

Barney took a deep breath.

"It's not just that," he began. Over the dishes it was suddenly easy to tell about his hauntings, about Great-Uncle Cole coming into his life and into his mind . . . "Not a ghost," Barney explained, "but a bit what a ghost would be like, if there were such thing as ghosts . . ." He told about Tabitha questioning him, and then going to Great-Uncle Guy, and he told his father Great-Uncle Guy's story about the Scholar magicians, and of the possibility that he might be a Scholar magician himself. His father listened without saying anything much. Barney could not tell what he was thinking or whether he believed what he was being told.

"Great-Uncle Guy said I gave out a sort of an electricity, just like Great-Uncle Cole used to do," Barney said. "And then he told Tabitha that he and Great-Uncle Alberic had found some letters from Cole at Great-Uncle Barnaby's house and that Cole wasn't dead after all, and what Tabitha and I think is that now Great-Uncle Barnaby's dead, Cole is lonely and wants me for a friend instead."

"Perhaps he likes the name," his father said grimly. "So that's why your Great-Uncle Guy thought it important to ring us up and tell us that he believed that this — this Great-Uncle Cole was still alive . . . It seemed a funny thing to do at the time."

Barney began to dry a knife very carefully.

"Cole thinks I'm his friend," he pursued, "because he thinks I'm the same sort of person that he is, but I'm not. I know I'm not. But he doesn't believe me."

"Are you absolutely sure that he isn't — well, another imaginary person?" Mr Palmer put his question very gently for fear of hurting Barney's feelings and making him fall silent. "I mean, you do have a pretty wild imagination, Barney. You could have invented another friend like Mantis and given him Great-Uncle Cole's name, because a lost great-uncle sounds rather — rather romantic."

"He doesn't feel like that at all," Barney objected, and shuddered slightly. "Well, perhaps he does, just a little bit, but much, much stronger. And he telephoned me . . . Mantis never telephoned."

"Telephoned?" repeated his father staring at him. So Barney had to tell about the footsteps suddenly falling silent, and the ring of the phone down the hall. As he talked he dried and dried the knife over and over again, until Mr Palmer quietly slipped it from his fingers. Barney glanced up to find his father looking at him with such an expression of concern that he nearly put his face in his hands and cried, just as Claire had done.

"This must be the driest knife in the world," his father joked a little. "Well, Barney — at least he

90

wants to be your friend. He's not an enemy. Don't worry so much."

But now Barney had to go on and tell the secret he had kept even from persistent Tabitha.

"He wants to take me away," he stammered. "He wants to take me away with him so that we will be magicians together. He thinks he's saving me. But I don't want to go."

"Good heavens!" muttered Mr Palmer. Then, more loudly, "Good heavens, I should say not. You belong here with us and no great-uncle magician, real or not, can take you from us. You're our boy, Barney. Don't ever forget it. No one can take you away."

"Real or not —" his father had said. He took Barney's story seriously, but he did not believe it was what it seemed to be. Barney thought that Great-Uncle Cole Scholar might be powerful enough to take him regardless of whether his father and Claire were willing to let him go, to take him and to wipe his memory out of the minds of his family and friends. Still he was glad to hear his father speak so strongly and definitely.

"Whether or not it's something you've thought up, or Cole Scholar is, or was, the greatest magician in the world, you're still our boy," his father repeated. "Do you hear me, Barney! Don't look doubtful! You're Dove's and my boy. You're Claire's and mine. We'd never let anyone take you."

Even when you half-know things are true, hearing them said makes them true all over again. Somewhere, in some cowardly part of his mind, Barney had feared that he might, he just might, what with the new baby coming and no more bedrooms in the house, be given away. He had thought that there might seem to be good reasons why he should be passed on to terrible Great-Uncle Cole. But his father's words filled him with confidence. He was happier than he had been for days.

Dishes over, he went out cheerfully, found it possible to laugh and have a loud, quarrelsome game of Fish with Tabitha, with both of them trying to cheat. At last he went to his bedroom having heard no footsteps, or received any messages since the phone call. He wondered if, perhaps, he was managing to put them out of his mind. There was no trace of Great-Uncle Cole in his mind.

When he switched the light on, the familiar things of his room met his eyes — his desk, planes, his pictures, his pillows, soft and plump, and his slippers beside his bed. Claire had straightened things out and made the room look welcoming to him. His book was on his chest of drawers and once he was ready for bed he went to get it and stood for a moment enjoying the backward look of his room reflected in the long looking glass. He looked only at the room for a while, not noticing his own reflection. When he did at last allow his eyes to meet the eyes of his reflected image he realized with a shock that the eyes he was looking into were not his own. They were round and golden-brown like his own eyes, but they were the wild owl eyes of Cole, the Scholar magician. As he looked further he saw that the face was not quite his own either— very like but still different, straighter eyebrows, more like Troy's than his, a dark watchfulness about the expression, a dangerous face, whereas he was sure his was not dangerous at all. It was not a wicked or a bad face, and at first Barney thought it was a face he liked, although it may have been only those parts of it most like his own face that made him feel this. Made brave by his father's certainty, by knowing for sure that he would not be given away, Barney stared back with curiosity. Then the lips moved and a voice, a child's voice but with that familiar huskiness still in it, spoke in his mind.

"Barney!" it said. "You see . . . we *are* brothers, brothers across time."

Barney felt his own face changing. Fear swept through him, now hot, now cold. Cole was close, close enough to change the image in the looking glass, to put his expression into Barney's reflected eyes. This creature, whose smile was so like his own smile, was a horror. He stood, while still awake, in the presence of a nightmare. Nor did it help that Cole was distressed by his fear.

"Please don't . . ." said the voice. "I'm only . . . I just wanted to . . . I'll go away now." There was a flicker over the surface of the glass and the reflection was Barney's own, reflecting a tormented face, twisted with distress into something ugly and almost as shocking as Cole's wild, impossible eyes.

Barney sprang into bed and pulled the blankets around him. His bed was wonderfully warm because, although it was a summer night, Claire had put a hot water-bottle into his bed, just as a sort of luxurious surprise. It was more welcome than she could have known, for Barney was shivering with cold fear. Not since the first haunting had anything frightened him so much. For now he felt himself to be nothing but a coat, a jacket that Great-Uncle Cole could put on or take off, could wear at will. Under the blankets, he felt as if he might, while shivering, still melt away with fear. The thought of darkness and sleep was terrible to him, yet he longed not to know anything about anything. He had told his story. People loved him and wanted to protect him, but nothing was changed. Hating the thought of losing any part of himself, he still longed for sleep, but sleep was not an obedient dog to come when you wished for it. Barney turned his face to the wall, wondered what he would say to Claire when she came up to kiss him good night, froze and melted at one and the same time and began his struggle with the long night.

9

A Black Hurricane in the House

Barney did sleep during the night, but not very well. The whole house seemed restless, and in his uneasy, half-awake dreams he heard footsteps up and down the hall, heard the telephone ring, heard voices. Once he thought he heard Claire's voice saying, "I don't believe it. They're all mad, but they're not going to make Barney mad, too. I won't let them."

When morning came he did not feel well. His head felt like a small airless room with someone inside it panting and beating a drum. Voices came and went in the usual morning way, but Barney lay still, thinking that perhaps he could no longer be seen or heard — that he was not a part of the house and family any more. Then Tabitha came bounding in, and he couldn't help noticing her notebook tucked into her dressing-gown pocket.

"I'm sick," he whispered, and she went bounding off again, shouting, "Barney's sick! He's really sick," as she ran down the hall. Claire and his father came in and looked at him.

"Get the doctor!" said his father.

"It's probably just 'flu," said Claire in a determined voice. " 'Flu and worry! Perhaps half an aspirin in honey, and a lemon drink. Don't worry, I just won't let it *be* anything but 'flu."

Barney smiled at her and later drank the lemon drink to please her. The curious thing was that he knew all the time that the headache was not his own. It was overflowing into him from Great-Uncle Cole. Somewhere in the early morning town Cole was wandering around looking at places he remembered, and something about the pattern of the streets, the old library, the town square was filling him with pain. He was not deliberately sending the pain on to Barney, but it was filtering through and giving him a headache because their minds were so close together.

Troy stalked in like some long, knobbly, black-maned giraffe and looked at him solemnly.

"It isn't fair," she said, more to herself than to him, and stumped out in her clumpy school shoes.

Barney felt the headache change from a headache of pain to a headache of sadness. Out in the town Cole was feeling unhappy about things that had happened many years ago, and — yes — for some reason he was frightened. The headache grew quieter and quieter. Barney went to sleep.

He woke feeling much better. Claire came and lay down for a while on the old bulgy couch in his room — "putting her feet up" — a thing that you have to do if you are going to have a baby. She was sewing a dress for the baby as she did this and talked about it to Barney. It was to be a boy, a brother, so that there would be two children of each kind in the Palmer family. Then she got up to make a cup of tea. Barney was allowed up too. Wearing his dressing-gown during the day gave him a special feeling of difference that he enjoyed.

Tabitha came home from school talking furiously about her class and her teacher. Troy came home and made another cup of tea. Then she sat in the cane chair in the corner half-hidden by the curtains and listened to Claire and Tabitha without saying anything herself.

"Hey!" said Claire. "What's going on? Usually Troy goes straight to her room and Tabitha makes herself half a dozen sandwiches and goes off swimming or visiting. Why are we all sitting around? What's up?"

"I don't know," Tabitha said. "I just thought you'd like the benefit of my company for a bit. It must be pretty dull for you while I'm away at school."

"Well, since you are around and about," said Claire laughing, "I might just run down to the shop to get some cream and a packet of peppercorns. You could keep an eye on Barney, couldn't you?"

"He looks much better again," Tabitha said. "I wish he'd make up his mind." But Claire put her library book and her sewing on the table and went out into the kitchen. For a few minutes the Palmer sitting room was quiet and restful, for Tabitha began to read and Barney and Troy were silent over their own thoughts. There came a knock on the back door. Barney felt it as if it were right inside his head, coming out of his ears instead of in at them.

"Come in!" shouted Tabitha carelessly.

"Don't!" Barney whispered urgently, but it was too late. There had been an invitation offered to the person at the door. They heard the door into the porch room open, then the sound of footsteps. The handle of the sitting room door turned. The sitting room door opened. Great-Uncle Cole came into the room. Tabitha leaned forward, her mouth open, Troy drew back, and Barney stayed still.

He knew he was seeing Great-Uncle Cole for the first time— not as a vision, not as a dream or a ghost, but as a real man, a man of about fifty years old, not so very much older than his own father. There were no shadows on the smiling face. It was plain to see in the broad light of the summer day, and this time it could be seen by other people, too. It was no longer Barney's exclusive vision. The golden eyes were the same fierce owl-eyes that had looked out at Claire and Tabitha through Barney, but they were now framed by silver-rimmed glasses. The brown hair was rather long, but it did not flow like magician's hair. Great-Uncle Cole was almost ordinary. Barney was astonished to find himself smiling back as if he were meeting an old friend. He was surprised to find he quite liked Great-Uncle Cole. At the same time he was afraid of him.

"I'll look like that when I'm grown-up," he thought, "but not exactly like that." The part of Great-Uncle Cole that frightened him was something that did not show very clearly on his face, nor could Barney tell exactly how he recognized it. He only knew that Great-Uncle Cole looked like a grown-up child.

There was still something in this man that frightened him, though. It lay in him like a clenched fist, folded in tight when it should have been open to the world. Something that should have grown freely had been stunted in this magical man, this owl-eyed enchanter. In some important way he was not much more than the fierce baby who had battled with his mother from the hour he was born, the child who had lived like a wild animal, refusing to speak in a house that was armoured to defeat him and to make him deny his special nature.

It was because of this dark childish part of him that Great-Uncle Cole, standing between them, was able to ignore, totally, Tabitha and Troy, and to speak to Barney as if he were the only person in the room.

"Here I am, you see," he said happily. "I'm not so very terrible, am I?"

Barney smiled back, cautiously, but with a real smile, not just a polite one.

"You didn't have glasses in my dream," he remarked.

"Beshrew me!" exclaimed Cole lightly. "I'm as blind as a bat without them. Isn't it funny? I can heal cuts and scratches, you know, but I can't do anything about shortsightedness. I don't know why, yet. Of course I can never tell exactly how a haunting will turn out because so much depends on what's already in the mind of the person I'm sending to. You'll find out."

"No!" said Barney. "Not me! It's all a mistake about me."

Great-Uncle Cole *did* seem to be a little puzzled by Barney.

"You *are* different from what I thought you would be," he admitted. "When I first knew about you— it was about three or four years ago— you were so strong. It was like a line of fire, a shooting star going across my sky. Like an arrow through me! I asked Barnaby about your family then, and he said that there *was* a boy, but not a magician, he didn't think. However, I *couldn't* be mistaken. It happened again and again, until about a year ago and since then, nothing but little flickers. But you know what they say, Barney, it takes one to know one. I *knew* you and I can't pretend to unknow you now. All I can think is that somehow your family is destroying your gift — oh, not deliberately — perhaps even through kindness. I just can't tell. But I think it *is* dying and I want to save it for you."

This was too much for Tabitha.

"Hey!" she cried indignantly. "That's us you're talking about. We wouldn't destroy his gift. If he were magic we'd all say, 'Go on, be a magician, don't let us stand in your way,' and we'd get books out of the library to help him and things like that. We'd never destroy his magic, if he turned out to be a magician. Not that he is," she added, giving Barney a patronizing glance.

Cole turned to her as if he had just noticed she was there.

"I'm not suggesting any of you would do it on purpose," he explained. "Just think for a moment,

Tabitha — you *are* Tabitha aren't you? — you could be a clever gardener, for example, and still pull up beautiful flowers if you didn't realize what they were. Unless you recognized them, they might just as well be weeds. That's what's happening with Barney. Believe me, I mean to help not harm him! I want to save him."

"No you don't," said Tabitha quickly and rather rudely. "You're just frightened of being lonely, even *I* know that. Why didn't you do something about him before if you wanted to help him? You didn't, did you? It's just yourself you want to help, not Barney."

"There's nothing magic about me," said Barney stubbornly. "If I was magic I'd know about it, but I'm not."

"Is he electric, for example?" Tabitha asked. "Great-Uncle Guy said *you* were electric when you were little. He said you could be felt in the whole house like electricity. Barney's not like that, is he?"

Great-Uncle Cole showed doubt. His eyes flickered a little. He stopped smiling and he looked up into the air around him, studying it for the answer to a diffcult question.

"The funny thing is, he doesn't seem to be," he said at last, "and yet this whole room is shining with his electricity, as you put it — the curtain rods, lampshades, even the table." He hesitated, while Tabitha looked incredulously around the room, and particularly at the table, battered by years of dinners, homework, games of cards and Monopoly.

"That table!" she exclaimed. "It doesn't shine, even with polish."

"To me it shines," said Cole. "A Scholar can see it." His puzzlement deepened. "Believe me, this whole room is reflecting power from somewhere. Something is really burning with the light of the Scholar magicians. It has to be Barney! Has to! But I can see he's learned what I've never learned — how to hide himself."

He turned to Barney and his eyes glowed as if they were indeed reflecting a strong light from somewhere, a light that fed their brightness but did not dazzle them.

"Barney," he said, "we have been companions now for about five days. I have been closer to you than anyone else in your life. I am your reflection — remember? — and you are mine! Just let go of all this — we can be off and away and there's no one to stop us."

He showed, by a wave of his long hand, that, by 'all this', he meant the old table, the green curtains, the worn carpet and the chairs (each one with it's own personality, from the uncomfortable straight one with the carved bird on the back to the big soft armchair Barney was sitting in himself). He meant all the other things that were 'home' to Barney, including Tabitha and Troy, his sisters. Tabitha leapt up.

"You're not touching him!" she cried, but to Cole she was nothing more than a moth that could be brushed away in an instant. At the same time Barney felt something begin to build up in Cole. A spiral of power began to spin as if he were winding himself into some kind of a fury. Barney clutched the arms of his chair, even though they were too wide to be properly clutched. His finger nails made a tiny scratching sound that seemed loud to them all.

"I can't let go, because I don't want to go," he said looking obstinately at the floor.

"Good on you, Barn!" cried Tabitha, while Barney searched desperately through his mind and memory to see if there was not, after all, some little bit of magic he could find to protect himself and his sisters. If there had been anything at all, he thought, he must have found it, but there was nothing there but ordinary happiness and sadness that could have belonged to anyone.

Cole's smile was certainly chilling this time.

"You may *have* to," he said very softly. The word *have* fell like a drumbeat, muffled but commanding, on the ears of Barney, Tabitha and Troy.

"Well, as far as I'm concerned," said a new voice butting in, "no one *has* to do anything in this house unless there's a good reason for it. Before Barney has to do anything for you, I, for one, will want to know your reasons, Mr Cole Scholar." It was Claire, standing in the open doorway, her shopping bag dangling limply over her arm. She was just in time, thought Barney, still aware of the spirally winding power building up in Cole. Another moment and he might have become a black hurricane and blown the house to pieces and carried off Barney like a hunter carrying off his prey.

Claire's voice came bright and sparkling with anger, and the black hurricane quietened before it. Great-Uncle Cole stood still for a moment, and then turned, smiling, to face Claire.

10

Magicians Revealed

"I know who you are, but what are you doing here?" asked Claire fiercely. "How dare you come into my house like this?"

"I was invited," Cole pointed out quietly. "I knocked and they asked me in."

"I didn't know it was *him*," Tabitha cried. "Really I didn't, Claire."

"I didn't either," Barney added, for Tabitha sounded so guilty and anxious.

"I would have come anyway," Cole said. "Why not?"

"I'll tell you why not . . ." Claire hesitated. "Because . . . because, I haven't worked out *how* yet, but somehow — you've been frightening Barney to death. He told his father last night that you were haunting him and then your brother, Guy, came around and told us — told us such a tale — well, I couldn't believe it. I *don't* believe it. This whole story about the Scholar magicians . . ."

Cole, who was only an inch or two taller than Claire, moved quickly and gracefully, placing a hand lightly over her fierce mouth, surprising her into silence.

"Shhhhhh!" he said, speaking in a mocking, affectionate way as if he were talking to an enemy of whom he also happened to be quite fond. "Don't! You're going to ask me to prove it, aren't you? But don't! Just ask Barney. He's a reliable boy, isn't he? Then ask him, and believe what he says."

"It *is* true Claire." Barney cried hastily. "He is a magician."

Claire's blue eyes looked over the top of Cole's hand at Cole's smiling face and then slid around to Barney's anxious one. Two pairs of golden eyes, one pair wild, one pair pleading looked back at her. She caught Cole's wrist and pulled his hand away.

"Barney is *very* reliable," she snapped, "but he's only eight. He's a child — easily tricked. And you have the cheek to tell me that I musn't ask you for proof. You can't expect me to believe something fantastic on the word of a frightened child. And I don't believe any of it. It's a Scholar family nightmare you've all got yourselves into and I certainly don't see that it's got anything to do with my Barney."

"*Your* Barney?" Cole's eyebrows shot up. "Yours?"

"He's mine all right!" Claire replied. "Everyone in this family belongs to everyone else— belongs *with* everyone else, rather. I've looked after him for a year now — ironed his shirts, made his school lunches, told him stories. I made that dressing-gown he's wearing, whereas no one even knew you were alive this time last week. But what matters most is that he *wants* to be ours and he doesn't want to be yours. That's what counts."

"But look at us!" said Cole. "Barney and I —

we're almost like the same person seen at different times during the same life. Don't we look as if we belong together? Besides, the proof you're asking for is difficult in some ways."

"I'm sure it is," said Claire sarcastically, "because I'm not a child. I won't be taken in by masks or faked footsteps or any of the tricks you've used to frighten Barney, and even Tabitha, from what I can make out."

Barney could feel Cole's black anger lift a stormy head, but when he answered, Cole's voice was light, cheerful, even careless.

"Oh, I can do it," he said. "I can prove over and over again the nature and capacities of the Scholar magicians — and you won't have any doubts about them at all." His owl-eyes wandered speculatively around the room and saw Claire's library book and sewing bag on the table. He picked up the book casually, shaking his head at Claire as he did so. "But you might hate the proof, you see. You might rather have it remain non-proven. Because that's the trouble! If it's pretty, if it's gentle, people think it's a trick. And if it's a strong proof, then they're frightened." He opened the book absentmindedly without looking at it, his eyes still on Claire. "And no one enjoys that! Of course, if they're frightened enough, they believe, but then they hate me. I don't want to frighten anyone and I don't want to be hated."

"As it is you've got a funny way of making yourself likeable," Claire retorted. "I'm not easy to frighten. Even if you were to show me my worst dreams I . . ." She automatically glanced down at the open book Cole was holding out to her, then stopped abruptly in the middle of her sentence, staring at the book in horror.

Tabitha, Troy and Barney could not see the pages that Cole was showing her or guess what had struck Claire to silence, though Barney, who was nearest to her, could glimpse some sort of a picture — a picture that flickered and moved. Claire continued gazing at the opened page, her eyes growing rounder. She shuddered all over and as she did so, two things happened. Cole leaned over and whispered something in her ear, and at the same time something dark and hairy with many legs and snapping jaws scuttled out of and across the pages to spring at her face. Claire screamed and struck the book out of Cole's hand, the spiderlike creature seeming to vanish in midair. The pages that the fallen book had turned up to the room were perfectly ordinary printed pages of a book. Barney leaped forward and hurled himself at Cole, attacking him with his fists. Tabitha, bewildered, for once did nothing but stand with her mouth open, but Troy was across the room in a moment, putting one arm around Claire's shoulders and a hand over her eyes as if to protect her from some horrible sight.

"You see?" shouted Cole, not laughing anymore, holding furious Barney off at arm's length. "You always ask for proof, you people, but you hate it when you get it. I told you — I warned you — but what I did was only what you asked me to do."

Claire was herself again within a minute. She

gently pushed Troy away, caught Barney to her side and said in a voice, still shaking, but commanding, too, "Don't! Stop it, Barney! He's right. He only did what I asked him to do. He gave me a proof I have to believe in." She looked at Cole bravely. "You're a mind-reader, then?"

"That's part of it," Cole said. "I can go into minds, read thoughts and memories, and I can also transform."

"But what did he do?" asked Tabitha. Claire sighed.

"He showed me one of my dreams — not a nice one," she said at last. "It was a dream I had had when I was about Barney's age, something that terrified me so much I could never bring myself to talk about it. There's always something that you can't tell, isn't there? I saw it all over again on that book and then, just as that — that thing jumped at me, Cole repeated words that were spoken in my dream, and the funny thing is that I had actually forgotten the words until I heard them again, just now."

"What were they?" demanded Tabitha greedily, half reaching for her notebook, but Claire laughed a little and shook her head.

"No!" she said. "Not now! Some other time, Tabitha."

Tabitha turned the power of her curiosity on Cole.

"Can't you do anything nice?" she asked, "or does it have to be horrible?"

"I can do many nice things," Cole said. He was

breathing rather quickly, and at the moment actually looked more alarmed and upset than Claire. "I can do many nice things, but people are never convinced, never compelled by them. However — watch!" His smile began to return uncertainly and he started to drum with his fingers on the edge of the table. Like a tiny echo, stronger and stronger, came the music of a different drum. A flute joined in, then a trumpet, a trombone and a violin. Out of Claire's sewing bag marched a little orchestra of mice, like the illustration from a child's picture-book come alive. The faces of Tabitha, Barney, Claire and Troy grew softer watching the parade dance around the edge of the table, piping and fiddling until at last they went back into the bag, whisking their long tails and laughing with a sort of squeaky mouse-laughter.

"How can it be true?" Tabitha cried, but Barney already knew that part of Cole's magic lay in having power over dreams. He had frightened Claire by showing her her nightmare, now he was enchanting her by constructing a happy dream for her so that, for a moment, she had forgotten he was dangerous and intent only on his own purposes.

"Mice in my sewing basket!" she exclaimed trying to sound cross, but Cole caught up a fold of blue material, tugged, and pulled out the baby's dress Claire had been sewing. He shook it. It seemed to flicker in his hands and when he held it up, its hem was wonderfully embroidered with flowers and ferns and with laughing mice who played the drum, the flute, the trumpet, the trombone and linked their tails in curling patterns. He held it out to Claire.

"For your daughter," he said.

"My daughter!" Claire exclaimed. "My . . ." She took the dress with one hand while the other touched the bulge where the baby was happily growing. Her voice died away and her face grew still and mysterious with an expression Barney had not seen before, a very private expression as if, for a moment, she and her baby were alone together in an empty room.

"Is it really . . ?" she began.

"Really!" Cole said. "I can hear *her* dreams too, you know."

Claire had started off being fierce and had then been frightened. The dancing mice had given her pleasure, but now she was frightened again — afraid of Cole in very much the same way that Barney had been frightened by him when Cole had taken over his reflection only last night.

"Please go!" she said. "Please leave us alone."

"I can't go without Barney," said Cole. "He'll waste away to nothing with you."

"You may be magical," Claire told him, "but you're mad. Mad to think you could come in to our house and take a child like that! We'd never let you have him."

Cole pulled his glasses down on his nose and looked at her over them. It was a comical gesture but he did not look comical. "Then I may have to take him whether you agree or not," he said.

At that very moment there was a distant clink from the catch of the gate, voices, and the sound of footsteps. One pair of feet separated themselves from the others and ran up the path. The porch door opened in an urgent way. Then the sitting room door burst open and Mr Palmer was with them, home an hour earlier than anyone could have expected him.

"Claire?" he cried. "Are you all right? Is Barney ok?"

"We're fine so far," said Claire as he put his arms around her. "But how did you know?" she asked. "How did you know we needed you?"

"I got a call," her husband replied. "Not the sort of thing I'm used to, but there was no mistake about it. Someone whispered in my ear that Barney needed help, even though there was no one there to do the whispering." Cole glanced at Barney who could only shake his head. "But I don't think I was the only one to get that call," Mr Palmer went on. "I haven't been able to work out why yet, but I think we're going to get visitors."

They all heard the porch door open again and slower footsteps, several of them, coming over the porch floor.

"Who?" asked Claire.

"A family party!" her husband replied reflectively, looking at Cole over Claire's head. "Mr Cole Scholar, I presume. Congratulations on not being dead, Uncle Cole, but within a minute you may wish you were. Sit tight, kids."

The sitting room door opened and in came the Scholar grandparents — but not alone. Between them leaning both on Grandpa Scholar's right arm and on her famous walking stick with the silver dog's head, was Great-Granny Scholar, like a meticulous, angry doll.

Just as Cole had been, she was interested in only one person in the room, but it was not Barney this time . . . it was Cole himself. Her black eyes fastened on him with a greedy hatred, a gaze that seemed to want him and to reject him at the same time

"Claire, my dear." Grandma Scholar was ruffled and upset. "I'm so sorry intruding on you like this. I don't know what you must think of us— first Sunday and then again today — but *she* suddenly insisted. Out of the blue! She got so— well almost hysterical, so absolutely determined that we should drop everything and rush to your house that I really thought she might make herself ill. We just — "

"Janet," said Grandpa Scholar. "There's Cole."

Grandma Scholar's eyes wandered around the room a little madly and discovered Cole standing by the table. "Oh, Cole!" she said in a changed voice. "Oh Cole, you're so *old*. Dear me — what a thing to say, when I'm so much older than you, but really, dear — almost like a ghost."

"Janet — lovely to see you again," Cole replied very politely. "You're looking well, Ben. And you, too, of course, Mother."

He sounded quite lighthearted, even amused, but Barney realized that Cole was alarmed — more than alarmed. Confronted by his brother and sister-in-law and most of all by his terrible old mother, Cole was afraid, choked with bad memories, fighting

113

against them and allowing the black tempest to rise in him again. Barney saw it in his own mind as a spinning cloud whirling, swelling outward, filling Cole's head as thick smoke fills and darkens a lighted room, making all things in it invisible.

"Looking well indeed!" said Great-Granny Scholar through false teeth that were rather too large for her and made her look more witchy than ever. Her voice was small and crackling. "Looking well! Is that all you have to say to me? Why have you come back? What are you doing here?"

"I wanted to visit Dove's children. Why not?" Cole replied.

"Why not, indeed, Cole," said Grandpa Scholar. "We're glad to see you." But Great-Granny Scholar was looking sideways at Tabitha, Troy and Barney, who sat silently on the sideline.

"So that's it," she hissed. "You want the boy, don't you? You know he's got the same wicked power that you've got and you want him to be your follower. I understand it all now. You're bad, Cole, bad. Why wasn't it you that drowned all those years ago instead of that other boy? There's no justice in the world."

There was an immediate outcry in which all adult voices merged in an untidy chorus. Barney could hear Grandma Scholar saying, "Don't talk like that, Mother. You'll only be sorry for it tomorrow."

"Sorry!" Great-Granny answered her bitterly. "Don't use that word to me, Janet. I'm not one of your weak, whining 'sorry' people. I'm too old to be sorry for anything now." Her bitter anger came into

Barney's mind with a sourer wind and a meaner chill than anything Cole could produce, beating back Cole's dark hurricane, causing Barney to stare at his great-grandmother with astonishment. A new, impossible idea about her began to flicker faintly as if he were adding his own little far-off lightning to the storms.

"That's enough!" said a new voice, but Barney could not tell if the words were spoken or were only somehow thought into his mind. He certainly seemed to be the only one who heard them, for the grown-ups did not react, so confused and angry were they. Now, like a snarling dog, Cole bared his teeth at his mother.

"You've been sorry for one thing," he cried. "You've been sorry that you ever had me. But I'm not going to die to please you, Mother dear. I'm not going to fade away. I'm going to take Barney and make him into a magician like me. I'm going to tear you into a thousand pieces and strew you all over the world to turn into a thousand little deserts where nothing will grow, and I'm going to wipe all memory of you and me and Barney out of every mind that ever knew us. I'm going to remake the world so that we can live in it and never be seen. I can do that you know, and more."

"Do it then!" his mother screamed, shaking, but not with fear. "You *freak*! You monster! But I'm not afraid of you. It's you who are afraid of me. Deep down you're too soft, Cole. You only *dream* of doing such things. You don't *do* them, or you would have done them by now. You'll always be afraid of me. I may not be magical, but I'm stronger than you."

Barney could bear it no longer.

"Don't!" he shouted to Cole. "Don't hurt anyone. I'll come! I'll come!"

"Barney!" His father caught his arm and held it tightly.

"That's *enough*!" said the new voice again and someone stood up and moved into the room. This time everyone heard it, for it was stronger than Cole's husky voice or Great-Granny's little gimlet tones. Everyone turned to look at the speaker. It was Troy.

"It is *not* enough . . ." began Great-Granny, glancing at her contemptuously, but was interrupted.

"How dare you!" Troy said. "How dare you speak to anyone like that. He's worth ten of you, you old bully."

Great-Granny tried to give Troy a chilling glance.

"It is no business of yours," she creaked out. "A child like you — you wouldn't understand."

"Oh yes I would!" Troy retorted and added mysteriously, "Remember Elizabeth's hair, Grandmother, and the wicked girl who set fire to it. I know all about that and other things, too."

Something had been said that changed the whole nature of events in this family sitting room. Cole stepped back a little, giving Troy a curious glance, hesitating to release his storm on the people in the room. Other assorted Palmers and Scholars looked

116

bewildered, but Great-Granny tottered as if Troy had pushed her and then stared, as if, before her very eyes, Troy had become a serpent talking with a human voice.

"I promised myself I'd never — no I'd never — I promised myself I'd say nothing and do nothing no matter what happened," Troy went on, stammering a little but sure of herself and of what she had to say. "I promised I wouldn't let myself be known. I've sat and sat and never said a word. Not one! For years I've come and gone and hidden in my room. But now I've got to tell." She looked at her father. "*I* called you to help Barney," she said, "but I didn't call *her*. How do you think she knew Cole was here? Why do you think she hates his magic so much that she can't bear it in the same town with her? It's because she's one herself, that's why. She was born a magician and once, when she was quite young, she did a dreadful thing with it and it scared her. She was jealous of her sister Elizabeth's hair and she set fire to it. Ask her if it isn't true. And after that she set herself to crush the magic right out of her life, to wipe out her own specialness. She put a false order on things around her. She tidied, tidied, tidied and turned all wild games into her sort of chess. It worked, too. Her magic died, but other good things died with it because it was her own specialness she killed. The really awful thing is she knows what she's lost and she can't bear to see it in anyone else — it drives her mad to think others might welcome it and enjoy it." Troy turned to Cole. "All those years you thought she was fighting you she was fighting herself just as much. I can't bear to think of it, it was all so *stupid*."

The old woman bowed down before Troy's torrent of scornful words but then, when Troy ran out of things to say at last, she reared up again.

"And just how do you know all this?" she asked in a bitter mumble. "How do you know about Elizabeth's hair? How do you come to know so much about me?"

"Because I've got some of your memories in me," Troy said. "You've never told anyone, but I can *remember* you doing it. And I have some of Cole's memories too. *I'm* not frightened to tell if I have to. *I'm* not afraid to be what I am." She turned back to Cole and looked straight into his owl-eyes. "There's no Scholar magician living in this house," she said, "but there is a Palmer magician, and it's not Barney. It's me."

11

"I'm Not Going to Be
the Same Troy"

Now Troy had begun talking it seemed that she could not stop. She was a torrent set free. Cole sank down on to the end of the settee beside Tabitha. Grandpa and Grandma Scholar gently helped the old lady back into an armchair, while Troy talked on and on.

"I've always known I was a magician and I always knew I had to hide it. Even when I was a baby, I knew it. And not only that, my mother told me to hide it— just before Barney was born, that was."

"Dove?" said her father, still standing in his own sitting room, with one arm around Claire and one hand on Barney's shoulder. "Dove knew? Dove told you?"

"Yes — one morning when I was nearly five — just before Barney was born. You had gone to work, and she took me into bed with her and said that she was going away for a while, and that when she came back I'd have a new baby brother. And then she said that if she didn't come back, for a while I was to be very careful. What she said was, 'You know that golden part of your mind, Troy, that magical part? Well don't let anyone know it's there until you are quite grown up.' She told me that one of her uncles had had a golden part to his mind, and that he'd been made to suffer for it. She didn't realize that I already

119

knew a lot about Cole because I could remember him." Troy looked down at Cole. "She didn't realize that some of your memories had got into me. I've got memories from all the Scholar magicians, though when they're very old I can't always tell who they belong to or what they mean. What I remember most about you is the wooden toys you used to make and that Great-Granny was always finding them and burning them. Of course, when I was four I loved the memory of those toys."

Great-Granny Scholar sat with her head thrust out in front of her. Tears overflowed from her eyes and lost themselves in wrinkles, but they were not tears of sadness.

"There is only one way to make wooden toys," she said. "You get the wood, you cut it or carve it. You peg it, you paint it. And there they were one day — up and down the hall — wooden dragons and crocodiles and clowns and birds. I burned them many times and I'd burn them again."

Cole bowed his face into his hands.

"But how did Dove know . . ?" Her father looked at Troy, not believing her. "She didn't say a word to me."

"She was like Barney is," Troy replied. "A lot of the Scholars are like him. Great-Uncle Barnaby was! They catch other people's thoughts and feelings very easily, read minds just a little bit, I suppose. It's a sort of sympathy and the sympathetic Scholars tune themselves to what other people feel. That's why Cole could reach Barney so easily and that's why I could make those friends for Barney — Mantis and the rest. I thought back to the trouble those wooden toys caused and I thought I'd invent something for Barney to play with — but something that no one else could see. I made them for him, because I knew he was feeling a bit lost and unhappy." She glanced apologetically at Claire. "Of course, when you came and he grew happier, I stopped all that."

"It seems to me," her father said, "that we're all a little mad — a little confused. Barney and Cole have overflowed into us and we're ready to consider anything as possible."

"Not me!" said Troy. "Shall I show you?"

"No!" said Claire and Cole together, and as Mr Palmer looked from one to the other of them, startled, Claire added:

"It will change everything. If she *can* show us — if she does — she'll never be the same Troy again."

"It frightens people too much," Cole agreed. "People hate being frightened."

"Oh, let me!" begged Troy. "I'm not going to be the same Troy again, anyway. Let me be free! No nightmares, promise!" And she held out her arms, became a flowering tree, a flying bird, a burning girl, a creature made of stars. Her boundaries with the rest of the world ebbed and flowed. She shrank to the size of a seed, grew great and dim like a mist spreading through the room, blazed once more and then became Troy again . . . Troy in a room full of family, but a room so still that the very silence seemed to sing around them with a cricket voice, not heard with the ear but felt in the blood. Great-Granny Scholar spoke first.

"I've seen and heard enough and more than enough," she declared. "All my life I've fought against this freakishness, this wicked, unnatural power which can be overcome with a little strength of character, a little unselfishness. But I've lived too long — long enough to see my great-granddaughter rejoice in it. Don't expect *me* to change *my* views — and Troy — I never want to see you again."

"Well I feel quite differently," said Grandmother Scholar. "Dear Troy — don't worry. It can only be good for all of us for you to be free of that old silence and struggle. Be a magician with my blessing, my dear."

"Mine, too," said Grandpa Scholar, his kiss on her cheek made bristly by his short moustache. "We'll find a way to see each other even if . . . But we can't discuss all that now."

"I don't change my mind, Ben!" snapped Great-Granny.

"Well, it seems as if everyone in this family is special but me." Tabitha pushed back into the conversation in a very determined way. "Everyone else can be a magician or be haunted, and that leaves just me stuck with ordinariness, though I was the one who didn't want it in the first place. I'm so ordinary that I should be Great-Granny's absolute favourite from now on, and she can leave me her fortune in her will."

"You've got your novel," said Troy. "You're going to be a world famous novelist, don't forget."

"I know, but it's such hard work," groaned Tabitha. "It's not fair!" She hugged her grandparents goodbye. "Do you want to be hugged, Great-Granny? I know you're pretty nasty a lot of the time, but I don't mind hugging you a bit because you're so little and miserable and nobody agrees with you."

"I don't need hugs," the old woman replied stiffly, as Tabitha put her arms around her. "I may be very old, but you can see I'm not weak. I'm not a rag doll."

"You're a great-grandmother of steel," Tabitha said, half admiringly, and a wintery smile touched the great-grandmother's mouth as if she could still be a little amused by a compliment.

"We'll come back soon on our own," Grandpa told them. "Don't vanish, Cole. We'll want to see something of you in — in more relaxed circumstances. I know Guy and Alberic will want to see you, too."

They left.

"How about a cup of tea?" said Mr Palmer. "Or even a whisky! Will things ever be reasonable again? And I'm hungry. Shall I cook dinner tonight? Cole — would you like to share a boiled egg with us?"

"We can do better than that," Claire cried. "I'll get some rice and . . ." She looked doubtfully at Cole who sat with his face in his hands and his shoulders hunched forwards in a cold, defeated way.

"Leave him be," her husband said, in a voice that sounded as if he might be sorry for Cole. "In its way all this must have been a shock for him. After years of being the only person who knew anything about — magic," he hesitated over the word, "— he's turned out to be nearly as wrong as anybody else. And perhaps the time's come for him to learn about something other than magic — to become more of a human being and not just a magician. It's something I've had to learn myself — to become a fuller person, I mean. And I'm lucky. I've had good helpers."

Troy gently shook Cole's shoulder. "He'll have good helpers, too," she said. Then she knelt down by Cole and spoke to him directly. "We've got a lot of talking to do," she said to him. "But there's no hurry. And it's not the end of the world to be wrong you know. People are wrong all the time in real life."

"I didn't even *think* of you," Cole murmured. "They said that only Scholar boys became magicians. I thought it had to be Barney."

"Who said so?" asked Troy. "*She* did, didn't she! She wanted to hide herself you see. Look — come for a walk and we'll talk, and then perhaps we could come home and have something to eat. Would that be ok, Claire?"

"Quite ok," Claire said. "We probably all need a break from one another. But don't be late, Troy, or I'll . . ." She hesitated and laughed, not entirely happily. "I don't suppose I'll ever need to worry about you again, will I? I don't suppose I've ever needed to worry over a magician."

"There are always car accidents," Tabitha declared cheerfully. "A car could come around the corner and . . . wallop! You'd need a terrific magician to get out of that one. Cole said he couldn't do anything about shortsightedness, and I don't expect he's much good with broken bones either."

"Or eagles dropping tortoises," Troy added, looking amused. "That happened in Ancient Greece, you know. An eagle dropped a tortoise on some dramatist and killed him."

"No eagles or tortoises here," said Tabitha, "but a bit could fall off a plane."

Cole laughed.

"A walk — even a dangerous one — would be good." He stood up, looking somehow smaller than he had looked before. "And company will be good, too," he added. "And then — if you really mean it — a cup of tea. If you can bear to have me around."

"They'll have me to look after them," Troy pointed out, "and besides if they want to stay friendly with me they'll *have* to have you, and vice versa. If you really need company, that is."

She took Great-Uncle Cole out of the house and down the path. They heard the catch on the gate clink.

"One thing is certainly true," remarked her father heavily. "She'll never be the same Troy again."

"No — because she's going to talk a lot, like me, from now on," Tabitha said. "You can tell that, can't you? I wonder what things are going to be like in this house with two of us talking all the time. None of you lot will be able to get a word in edgewise."

12

Spinning the World

A week later Barney came in through the Palmer gate which clinked its catch at him in a cheerful voice. He had been to the swimming pool with Nick, a boy who had started school in Barney's class on Monday and who needed someone to show him around. Tabitha had refused to come with them, saying pompously that she had far more important *cultural* things to do these days than go swimming. As well as a world-famous novel, she was now planning to write a world-famous ghost story.

Claire was out in the garden pulling some things up and putting other things in, as gardeners do. Her hair was loose and she looked like a rather stout Alice-Through-the-Looking-Glass speaking severely to a border of daisies.

"Hi!" said Barney and she smiled an upside down smile at him under her arm, before she straightened up with a sigh.

"Oh dear — it's getting too much for us," she said. "For Emma and me, that is."

Emma was the name of the new sister. "She's kicking me in a very impatient way," Claire complained. "I think she wants me to go in and have a cup of tea."

"I'll make one," Barney offered. "Then you can

come in and sit down with Emma for a bit."

"Oh, would you? Thanks, Barney. After all, there's not much summertime left. It's a pity to waste these last days. Everyone's in there by the way . . . Cole, Troy, and of course, Tabitha, talking about goodness knows what."

Barney went in. Already Great-Uncle Cole's visits to the house were taken for granted. Barney wondered if Claire realized that Great-Uncle Cole was planning to live in their town permanently, so that he would never be far away from the Palmer family and Troy ever again. It was as if he were learning something about his own childhood through watching the Palmers reading, playing cards, arguing over whose turn it was to wash up, and doing their homework. But in return Tabitha was studying Great-Uncle Cole. In the sitting room Barney found Cole and Tabitha sitting at the table which looked as if it was covered with Tabitha's notebooks. He could see the word *Stepmothers* written down the spine of the one nearest to him. However, he knew that Tabitha had bought a new notebook which was to be devoted especially to Great-Uncle Cole and it was marked *Ghosts and Magicians*.

"The first ghost . . ." Tabitha was saying, writing away. "Why did you send that blue velvet boy to Barney?" She looked over the table sternly. "It nearly scared him to death. He came home and fainted on the front steps because he thought it was telling him he was already dead."

"It seems like something done by somebody else

in another time," said Cole. "Remember, I thought he'd understand what was happening and besides — really I didn't have a very clear idea of just how old he was . . . I thought he was about five and when I tried to remember being five myself, that picture was what I remembered. My brother Barnaby gave it to me — that picture and a lot of others with the scrapbook. You might think a magician wouldn't care very much about presents but it was very precious to me. Hello, Barney — have a good swim?"

"Yes, thanks!" Barney replied. Beyond the table, stretched out along the settee on her stomach, lay Troy, her chin on the end of the settee and her hair hanging down almost to the floor. She wiggled her right foot at Barney in silent greeting, as he went through to the kitchen to put on water to boil for tea. When he came back Tabitha was asking Cole about his life after he had run away from the old Scholar house.

"What did you *do*?" she asked. "Did you live by magic?"

"I did this and that," Cole said. "I worked in a hamburger bar, and then as a gardener in a park. I did a lot of different things. Sometimes I used magic to help me but only in small ways — only to do things people would believe in anyway. I got a job as a nightwatchman and I saved a little bit of money and took a course in graphic design. Now I work with an advertising firm and do stage sets for a theatre company, and I have a lot of fun one way and another."

"So you've done nothing much with your magic

really." Tabitha fixed him with a commanding eye.

"Only kept it secret," Cole replied, "and shared it a bit with Barnaby."

"And haven't you got any friends?" asked Tabitha incredulously.

"Oh, I know a million people," said Cole. "But no one knows me. That's why brother Barnaby was so precious to me. We really knew each other. No need to explain, to hide, to pretend anything was what it wasn't. He never ever tried to keep me out of his mind. I could talk to him any time of the day or night, even though it meant he had no secrets, poor fellow. Mind you, he liked the feeling of tricking our mother — the feeling of leading a life that she knew nothing about. He would warn me when she was around and I'd keep away. Funny! Here I am, in the last two weeks, suddenly closer to more people than I've ever been in my life before. Troy says I have to learn a lot and that being part of a family will help me learn it."

"How to be more of an uncle and less of a magician, I suppose!" Tabitha said.

"How to be a great-uncle and a magician as well," Barney suggested kindly.

"My idea," said Tabitha leaping to her feet, "is that I take you down to the shops and you buy us ice-cream for our dessert. I'll help you choose. That's a good uncle-ish thing for you to start on. Ice-cream could be your family project for the day, because I happen to know there's only stewed fruit for dessert tonight, and Claire never puts enough sugar in it."

Cole groaned, but got up smiling.

"Don't laugh!" he said over his shoulder to Troy, who looked up at him gravely through her black hair.

"I'm not!" she replied, and indeed there wasn't even the hint of a smile on her face.

"You can't fool me," said Great-Uncle Cole. "You and I both know that there are more ways of laughing than anyone supposes."

"And I'm going to learn them all," replied Troy, "and so are you."

"Yes, ma'm." Great-Uncle Cole nodded and followed Tabitha out with a meek step and a mischievous smile.

Troy and Barney were left alone together. Slowly, almost unwillingly, their eyes met.

"Isn't it funny," said Troy slowly, "how a few days can change things?"

"Two weeks . . . well almost two weeks," Barney pointed out. "Quite a long time, really."

"Dad will never feel easy with me again," Troy went on, almost absentmindedly. "Do you realize that? He tries to think of me just as he used to, but he can't. Too much to expect, I suppose. I can feel him looking at me and — I don't know — shrinking away from me."

"He does, a bit," said Barney. "I know he does. He might get over it."

"He'll get better if I'm careful," Troy said, "but he'll never get over it altogether. I knew it would be like that, but still . . ."

Barney had nothing to say because he knew Troy

did not need him to say anything.

"But it's lovely to have met Cole at last," Troy went on, more to herself than to him. "It's nice to have someone you don't have to explain to. When I've finished school — when I'm a bit older, we're going to set out to find other magicians. There must be others somewhere. And then we'll . . ."

"What?" asked Barney, not because she wanted to be asked, but because he wanted to know.

"Well, we'll change the world, won't we?" Troy pointed out. "Make it better in some way."

"How better? What ways?"

"I don't know . . . better . . . different. That's all I know at present."

"Better for everyone or just better for you?" Barney asked suspiciously.

"I don't know," said Troy impatiently. "Look, for years it's been all covered tracks, closed doors for me. I've been a bit like Great-Granny — you know — tidy, tidy, tidy, concentrating on some outside pattern so that my inside pattern wouldn't get too strong and show itself to everyone. It's only a few days ago that I was free to think about what to do next, but there must be something to do." She smiled mysteriously into the air. "It wants to show itself. It wants to be recognized . . ."

"What does?"

"The magic does, idiot. Here, do you realize that kettle's boiling? It's been boiling for about two minutes."

Barney went into the kitchen and made a pot of

tea. Then he ran out into the garden to get Claire, and they came back together. Troy was still lying stretched out on the settee, staring over the end of it apparently at the floor. But between her long nose and the floorboards was an odd darkness, a patch of night into which she was gazing as intently as a gypsy fortune-teller might gaze into a prophetic crystal.

Claire and Barney watched her curiously.

Something began to move in her patch of darkness. A tiny sun no larger than a mustard seed danced around on an axis of fire. Planets moved around the sun like grains of dust. Troy was casting dreams of the solar system into this darkness she had magicked up in the Palmer's homely sitting room. The sun sank away and one of the planets grew larger — a planet with one moon, a planet of continents and oceans, streaked and swirled with masses of cloud. Apart from the clouds it was very like the globe of the world that stood on the filing cabinet in Barney's classroom. Troy studied it somberly. Then slowly she put out one long finger and gave it a little push.

"Faster," she said, and behold — it spun faster. She smiled darkly to herself.

"Slower!" she said and it slowed down.

Barney and Claire continued watching not so much the planet as Troy's face with it's high cheekbones and its long, lowered lashes. She looked up and saw them watching her. At once the darkness and the spinning world vanished and Troy sat up, her pale face unexpectedly reddening with a shame Barney only dimly understood.

"It was only a game," she said to Claire, who hadn't said anything.

"A dangerous game!" Claire replied, not smiling.

"But Tabitha plays it in a way — with her novel writing. Everyone does it — dreams of spinning the world." Troy shrugged her shoulders.

"But not everyone can," Claire said in a cool voice.

Troy leaped up and rushed over to Claire and flung her arms around her.

"Don't go all cold and disapproving! I can't bear it. I don't know what to do. It was easier when all I had to do was keep quiet and hide. Now it's all mixed up." Troy was actually crying.

Claire patted her back and said, "Troy — dear Troy, don't imagine things being any more complicated than they need be. Go on almost as you've always done — do your homework, pass your exams, and just concentrate on what you're doing: helping Cole, playing games, making jokes. One thing at a time. After that — we'll see. But, at present, please, for everyone's sake, be easy on yourself."

Troy sniffed a little.

"I know you're right," she said, "but — oh Claire, if only you knew — you are right though. Only one step at a time. Awful to overbalance now, having got this far." She grinned rather ruefully. "Actually I'm behind on my history — first time ever, I think, so I'll just . . ." She moved over to the hall door and was almost through it when she turned unexpectedly and gave both of them a straight stare.

"Not to make a great fuss about it or anything," she said, "but I do love you both." Then she slammed the door and a moment later they heard the click of her own door down the hall.

"The tea will be cold," said Barney.

"Oh, it'll be warm and wet," Claire assured him. "Look — it's still steaming." They poured their tea and sat on kitchen stools to drink it.

"I don't want to spin the world," Barney said. "I don't know what I want, but I do know it's not that."

"Nor do I!" Claire shook her head. "Poor Troy! If you can do almost anything, it's all the harder to choose the right thing to do. Poor Cole, too — coming in like a lion and then staying like a pet lamb. I suppose if most of us were asked, we'd think that magicians would be free of care, but somehow or other there are always rules."

"It's been good, though," Barney said. "I mean it's a bit like coming in after a stormy night and finding everything is safe and warm. Then you can sit down and start to enjoy the memory of the storm. You hate being in it, but it's nice to remember."

"And we're more of a family, too," Claire said. "We've all told one another things and come closer together "

"Troy's said too much for Dad," Barney pointed out. "She says he'll never get over it . . . he'll always feel a bit spooky about her."

"Yes — well, he might," Claire said, "but it will matter less and less as time goes by. He'll get used to the fact that he's got a Palmer magician around."

"And Tabitha will be a world famous novelist," said Barney.

"I'm very much afraid that she might be," agreed Claire with a grin.

"Claire," said Barney. "Claire, it isn't fair to have favourites in families is it? To have a favourite sister, I mean?"

"It isn't fair but sometimes it happens," Claire replied cautiously. "Why?"

"Don't tell anyone but Emma's my favourite," Barney whispered across the kitchen.

"Oh, well that's another story," said Claire, laughing. "We'll have to wait and see how she turns out."

"I know already," Barney said. "She's going to look quite a lot like you but she's going to have Dad's nose, so she's not going to be totally pretty — just nice and funny-looking and she's going to be interested in planes, like me, and —"

But Claire stopped him.

"Barney," she said. "I don't know if you really do know through some Scholar — no, some *Palmer* magic — or if you're just guessing, and I don't want to know. Just pour me another cup of tea and get yourself another biscuit and let's talk about gardening or planes or something quite different. After all — there have to be some surprises left for us ordinary people, don't there?"